LATIGO'S PURSUIT

ALSO BY PATRICK LINDSAY

Opening the Frontier: Spencer and Son

Latigo Series

Latigo's Choice: Taming the West

Latigo's Chance: Boomtown Gold

Latigo's Trouble: Meltdown in Leadville

LATIGO'S PURSUIT

ANSWERING THE CALL

LATIGO BOOK FOUR

PATRICK LINDSAY

WOLFPACK
PUBLISHING
— EST 2013 —

LATIGO'S PURSUIT

ONE
A REQUEST FOR HELP

NEAR SILVERTON, COLORADO, 1882

I t was late spring, which made it a little chilly to be out surveying my ranch property. Even so, I never get tired of doing this. My little spread up against the mountains of Colorado was a dream come true. I pulled up the collar of my sheepskin jacket and turned my horse Buck to climb an incline at the far end of my property. There was a wide shelf up there, winding around the mountain and overlooking my northern pasture. It was the best viewpoint to see how my cattle were surviving an unusually cold spring.

Buck scrambled up the slope. A little loose shale dribbled down the slope behind us, but he kept a firm footing. I paused him at the top and took out my binoculars to check the cattle I could see from my new lookout. I swung the glasses back and forth one time, then froze and focused in. There was a lone cow down, and from what I could see, she had been mangled.

A few possibilities raced through my mind, and I stowed away the glasses and reached for my Winchester. A predator had done this, I was sure, but where was he? The wind shifted and blew an icy blast down my collar. At the same time, Buck snorted and laid his ears back. I looked down the trail to see what he had reacted to.

I missed seeing the predator the first time I looked. It was the twitching tail that gave him away this time. I levered the Winchester as my eyes traveled up to see the powerful shoulders and pointed ears. *Mountain lion!*

Those eyes weren't blinking, and they were zeroed in on us. Buck would normally hold his ground if I fired from the saddle, but this wasn't normal. He could smell that cat, and he backed away, tossing his head and snorting. Should I dismount to get a better shot?

As it turned out, I had no choice. The mountain lion came off the ground with a snarl as Buck reared off the ground. I leveled the Winchester and snapped off a quick shot. A lucky shot, actually. The bullet caught him right-center in his chest. It wasn't a kill shot, but it threw him off balance and he tumbled down onto the rocky shelf. He wasn't dead—his paws scraped the shelf as he pulled himself up.

I kicked out of the stirrups and bailed out. I could hear Buck racing away, plunging down the slope behind me and heading for the pasture below. I levered the Winchester again as he snarled and gathered himself. I didn't know if he had enough left to charge me, but this was no time to take chances.

He came to his feet facing toward the pasture below, struggling to get his footing, but offering me the shot I needed. My second bullet went through his neck and dropped him back down on the shelf.

I stood rooted to the rocky shelf, watching him for any signs of movement. Sweat was trickling down my neck despite the icy forty-five-degree breeze. Finally, I turned my head to look for Buck. He had come to a stop maybe a hundred yards away and was grazing at what spring grass he could find out there.

I levered the Winchester one more time and approached the big cat, rifle aimed just in case he had something left. He didn't twitch as I got close. I slowly reached out and prodded him with the Winchester. Nothing.

I heaved a sigh and looked out at Buck again. "I don't suppose you'd cotton to me hauling him home, would you?" He couldn't hear me, but I knew the answer to that one. I would leave the mountain lion here.

Shouldering the Winchester, I retraced my steps back along the ledge and scrambled down to the pasture below. I heard my name being shouted as I reached the pasture and looked up to see my ranch hand, Otis, galloping toward me. No question he'd heard the shot. We had been checking this same northern pasture. I waved my rifle over my head to let him know I was okay. He slowed his pace and cantered up to me.

Otis had been with me for a few years now. We'd got off to a terrible start, I gotta admit. We had us a knuckle-and-skull fight in the main street of Silverton as a howdy-do. I shook my head at the memory. The first good punch he got in felt like I'd been kicked by a Missouri mule. Not that I've ever been kicked by one. It's how I imagined it would feel.

Anyway, Otis and I had settled our differences, and he came to work for me. I was lucky to have him. He leaned over in the saddle and shot a glance up the slope behind me. "What was it, boss?"

"Mountain lion." I jerked my head over my shoulder to show him the shelf up above.

His eyes widened as he looked up the slope, then he looked me over. I guess he was checkin' for some claw marks on my neck or a torn-up coat or something like that. I shook my head and held up my hand for him to swing me aboard his horse.

"I got him before he got me," I explained. "Nasty-lookin' cat, though. I was kinda wishing I had me a Sharps buffalo gun to take him down on the first shot."

We rode over to where Buck was still grazing, and I slid down from Otis's horse. "He got one cow, over yonder," I said, pointing. "Could you take care of that before you come back?"

Otis tipped his hat at me. "Shore thing, boss," he said lazily before riding away.

I looked over at Buck. "Yellow-bellied," I accused him. "You're just plain old yellow-bellied." He finished chewing and gave me a nudge with his nose, then drifted a few steps away, looking for some fresh grass.

I shook my head and shoved the Winchester back into the scabbard. "Can't blame you, old boy," I admitted. "I got me a Winchester. You ain't got nothin' but them legs to try and outrun him." I mounted up and turned for home.

Home was a nice ranch house I had bought along with the property, lock, stock, and barrel, from a man who needed to get his family to safety. I made him a fair offer, and he snapped it up. I had helped his family get safely aboard a train to start a new life. Now I was a lucky man to share this house and ranch with my wife, Joanna, and our baby boy, Ethan.

I groomed Buck and turned him loose into the corral, then picked up the Winchester and walked across the yard. Joanna came out to give me a kiss, holding baby Ethan. "Da!" he said, pointing at me.

"Don't you forget it, son," I advised him before taking him from Joanna and walking into the kitchen. Joanna gave me coffee and the breakfast she'd been keeping warm for me.

Joanna settled into the chair across the table, holding Ethan while I ate. "How did it look?" she asked. "The cows are healthy?"

I nodded. "Cows are doin' fine," I assured her. "They're finding some good grass in that upper pasture, early as it still is. I'll rotate 'em back down below before long."

She was watching me closely. That woman could read my mind like it was a book. Well, considering how long it took me to read a book, maybe she could read it better than that.

I went ahead and told her about the mountain lion, but I left out the part about how close I got to that beast before I saw him. And the part about my heart beating just about clean out of my chest. I left out that part, too.

She waited for me to finish breakfast, then shrugged. "Maybe you should keep Otis closer to you when you get up above that north pasture," she observed.

I nodded my head. That was a good idea.

I puttered around the house for a while, building up the fire in the stone fireplace and generally prowling around. After an hour, I watched while she put Ethan down for a nap.

She came out of Ethan's room and looked at me, knowing I was bored. "Why don't you go to town?" she suggested. "You could check in on Sarge and go over to the *Suds 'n Such* to see Holt."

My eyes lit up. Going to town meant going into Silverton. That was our town. Sarge was the sheriff there, and he was tougher than an old saddle. I was happy to have him on my side in any kind of fight, and we had been through a few of 'em together.

Holt was my partner in the *Suds 'n Such* saloon. We had hitched our fortunes together when I first came to Colorado, working for the railroad and building a future in this new land. I checked the clock in the corner. Almost noon. Not too soon to share a beer with Holt.

I kissed Joanna, grabbed my hat, and went outside to saddle Buck again. I swung aboard and turned out of the corral, feeling a snowflake brush my cheek when I reached the trail to town. I shook my head and looked up to see a few more flakes drifting down. It looked like I would have to bring those cows back down to the lower pasture sooner than I'd thought. Spring was slow to come this year.

The sights and smells were all familiar when I pushed the doors open and walked into the *Suds 'n Such*. The room was almost empty, but my old friend and partner, Holt Burns, let out a beller when I walked in. We had started out with a 60-40 split of the profits here, but I wasn't around much anymore, so now I only took twenty-five percent and helped keep an eye on things now and then.

Holt pulled me a beer and sailed it down the bar at me. I grabbed it just before it sailed past and took a deep pull. I sighed and wiped my mouth with my sleeve. I squinted over the beer glass at Holt.

"Am I your first customer today?"

"Yup. What brings you in so early? Joanna kick you out?"

I chuckled. Holt knew better. "Nope, got done checkin' the stock, and what with a life-threatnin' attack from a mountain lion, I needed a beer."

"Really?" He studied my face suspiciously. "You sure it wasn't a barn cat goin' crazy or sumthin'?"

"Nope." I went on to tell him the story. Okay, I might have polished it up a little here and there. His eyes got a little big.

"Dang," he breathed. "Ain't you just a reglar Davee Crockett."

I tilted back my beer, stared sorrowfully into the

bottom of the glass, and stared up at Holt. "Did Dav-ee, uh, Davy Crockett kill mountain lions?"

"I dunno. Only name I could think of." He took the beer glass back behind the bar, did his magic, and served up another one.

I felt a little breeze at my back and Holt bellered again. "Dugan!"

Dugan was a giant of a redheaded miner. I had helped Dugan and his buddies when there were high-waymen stealing cash and ore from the miners around these parts. I had to put my beer down while Dugan came up behind me and tried to squash the life out of me. Finally, he let go and settled for a massive slap on my back.

"That beer's on me!" Dugan boomed, pointing at my glass. "And one for me." He parked himself on a stool next to me.

"Kinda early for you to come in here, ain't it?" I asked, checking myself over to see if he had busted any ribs.

"Goin' out on the trail today," he told me. "Found us a good vein of ore up there. Cashed some in this mornin', going right back. What've you been doin' out there at that ranch?"

"Been wrestlin' mountain lions barehanded," Holt announced.

Dugan stared at me suspiciously, so I told him the real story. I didn't even polish it up that much. I didn't need another bear hug.

Dugan shook his head when I finished the story, then picked up his beer to go join a couple mining buddies who had come in. "Hitting the trail soon," he reminded me. He turned back. "You know, Lat, you just gotta let me know if'n you ever have any trouble out at that ranch. Four-legged varmints or the two-legged kind, we'll come a runnin'."

We shook hands, and I went back to my beer. Holt came around the counter and joined me. His next visitor took us by surprise, seeing how early in the day it was. Sarge came through the door, spotted us, and came over. He was carrying a piece of paper and wearing a troubled frown.

"Have a set," Holt advised, pointing at a stool and setting down a beer.

Sarge mumbled to himself, took a sip, and growled at the paper he had been holding. He plunked it down in front of me.

"Got this off that new clickin' contraption they set up," he growled. "Pecks like a woodpecker and spits out paper."

"Telegraph machine," I told him. Silverton had one now. I could see that Sarge didn't think much of it. "What's this about?" I asked, picking up the paper.

"Stagecoach robbery, up north near Gunnison," Sarge said. "Your buddy Anderson, the marshal, thinks they might come this way. Askin' me to help if I can."

I smoothed out the paper and read what Anderson had to say, which wasn't much more than Sarge had already told me. Two stagecoach robbers had struck near Lake City, getting away with about one hundred dollars. Shots had been fired. The shotgun rider had been killed. Anderson thought the driver might have hit one robber with a shotgun blast.

I pushed the paper back over to Sarge and thought about it. Gunnison was a pretty new town, and it was booming on account of mining and railroads. This place, Lake City, must be really small. They probably didn't have a sheriff in the town. Anderson was probably short-handed himself, as usual.

Those things made sense to me. What didn't make sense was why Anderson thought they might come south to the Silverton area. There were plenty of places for a couple of outlaws to lie low up there.

Sarge was watching me over the top of his beer glass. "Whatcha think?" he asked.

I shrugged. "The only part I don't get is why he thinks they might come down here." I drummed my fingers on the bar top. "Have you heard about any cattle rustling going on up there? They have some big herds around Fairplay now. That's north and west of this holdup, but there's good ranching country all around. Sometimes those outlaws have their hands in just about everything—railroad robberies, cattle rustling, stagecoach holdups, you name it."

Sarge shook his head. "They've likely had a few cows poached here an' there, but no big rustlin' operation I've heard about. You know there's been railroad robberies. All that ore and payroll on the trains. I guess you know the Santa Fe folks have hired the Pinks to help out."

I nodded. The Pinkerton Agency had some detectives riding on the trains now, and those boys meant business. They might have scared some outlaws off train robberies and into other things.

Sarge broke into my thoughts. "Why'd you ask

about cattle rustling? What are you thinkin' about there?"

I finished my beer and waved Holt away when he came with a refill. I looked back over at Sarge. "If they've been doing some large-scale rustling up there, it might make sense they would try to drive them cows south, into New Mexico, and maybe even clear down to Mexico. Maybe Anderson thinks it's the same people who did the stagecoach robberies and it's all tied in somehow. They might come past Silverton with some rustled livestock."

I stood and put on my hat. "Maybe I'll go over to the telegraph office and ask Anderson some questions," I told Sarge.

"'Preciate it, pard," he said. He put out a hand to stop me. "I think I'm gonna have to go up there to Salida and look around," he said. "Can you spare a couple days to help? One day ride each way and a little lookin' around. You're the best tracker we've got," he reminded me.

I hesitated, then nodded. I was sure Joanna and the ranch could spare me for two or three days. Otis could look after things, and Holt was good about riding out to check on things at the ranch for me. He nodded at me now without being asked.

"My place, first thing tomorrow," I told Sarge. "I'll be ready to go."

———

I stepped over to the telegraph office and sent a

message to Anderson, letting him know I would help Sarge, and asking what else he could tell me about it.

After spending a couple hours picking up a few ranch supplies and having lunch, I went back to the telegraph office. I had my answer from Anderson.

There had been an increase in cattle rustling up around Fairplay, north of Salida, and Anderson thought the same gang might be behind it that had pulled off the stagecoach robbery. He had asked Sarge for help, hoping I would join in, and had supplied my name to the new sheriff in Salida.

I sighed and mounted up on Buck, turning him toward home. I had worked with Anderson to clean up Leadville a couple years ago, and my name had gotten around. I was really trying to step away from that and build up my ranch with Joanna. I wanted my days as a lawman to be over.

Buck struck the familiar trail home, and I barely needed to guide him. In the end, I thought, I mostly wanted our town and state to be a peaceful place, and I was helping a friend if I went with Sarge. That's how I would have to look at this.

TWO
LAKE CITY ROBBERY

W es Fulton jerked back and forth on his
mattress twice, muttering to himself. The
dream ended like it always did, with him coming wide
awake and sitting bolt upright. As always, sweat
poured down his face. He cursed, threw off his blanket, and walked to the door of his cabin. He stepped
outside, ignoring the cold wind blowing down the
ravine.

The dream always ended with him being lynched.
He knew why it ended that way—he had witnessed
that exact thing happening to his good friend, Ace
Musgrove. That was a name people knew around
these parts, and most would have said he got what he
had coming. Wes Fulton didn't see it that way.

Ace Musgrove had a gang operating in Colorado
and other places, mostly during and after the Civil
War. He was a cattle rustler, mainly, but he wasn't
above robbing banks and miners if he got the chance.

Fulton had joined the Musgrove gang shortly after

the war, and he had found a home there. He'd lied about his age to join the Union army in 1864, but the army wasn't what he had expected. He'd spent more time in the stockade than out. His stockade time, he had to admit, might have saved his life. Lots of folks died in the front lines. Still, after the war, he'd had enough of the stockades. Drifting to Colorado, he had found an older brother in Ace Musgrove, joining in on bank robberies and cattle rustling.

With some money in his pocket for the first time in his life and with his friends around him in the gang, Fulton thought he had found his home. The cash was flowing in, and the law was always a step or two behind. That all changed after the big train robbery they had pulled off in 1868. A posse had formed after that Colorado robbery and had chased down Ace Musgrove and a couple others from the gang. Wes Fulton had escaped mostly through luck—he had stayed behind to finish out his poker game when the others left the gambling house where Ace had been arrested.

They had taken Musgrove to jail in Denver, and Fulton had tagged along behind them with some idea in his head of busting Musgrove out of the jail before trial. Fulton had actually been stationed down the street, watching the jail, when the vigilantes came.

There were too many of them for Fulton, and they were heavily armed. Fulton knew he had no chance of freeing his friend, but that hadn't stopped him from trailing the vigilantes as they hauled Ace Musgrove away from the jail. He'd watched while they had strung up Musgrove and hung him from the Larimer

Street Bridge. It was the same image that kept popping up in his dreams.

Fulton was shivering now. The cold wind had dried the sweat on his face and neck. He stepped back into the cabin. He knew he had been lucky to find this abandoned cabin, tucked away in a narrow gorge under the overhang of a rocky ridge of the Mosquito Mountain range. He had moved in three weeks ago, and nobody had shown up to claim it. It made the perfect hideout.

Wes Fulton had three others in his gang at present, but they didn't know about this cabin, and he didn't plan to fill them in. When they met, they met in a saloon in the town of Fairplay. He might need this cabin any time now because there was nobody he dared to trust. The ridge above made a great lookout point, and there was a deep cave behind the cabin. Fulton was sure that the cave had been used as a hideout by somebody. That somebody had probably built the cabin in front of the cave.

Still shivering, he tossed some scraps of wood into the small log fireplace and warmed himself over the fire. Fulton sat down, huddled in front of the fire, and scowled at the memory of yesterday's robbery. He pulled aside the bandage on his shoulder and checked the wound left there yesterday when a shotgun pellet had hit him. Getting that pellet out of his own shoulder was something he wanted to forget.

Fulton went looking for his whiskey bottle. There were only two swallows left in the bottom of the bottle, so he made quick work of them. He reached for another stick to throw in the fire, cursing when there was a sharp pain in his wounded shoulder. That robbery yesterday seemed to have been cursed from the start.

Stupid idea from the start, if he was going to be honest. They had trailed a stagecoach south from Gunnison, thinking it would turn off to the east and toward the mining camps. When it kept going south, they knew it wasn't serving the mining camps. That meant no rich payload. Still, angry at wasting most of the day, they decided to rob this one for whatever it was carrying.

It had looked easy enough. There was a shotgun rider, which usually meant the stage was carrying a strongbox with something worth their time. The shotgun riders usually threw their hands in the air when they saw they were outgunned, but this fool had reached for his Winchester and got himself killed. The strongbox had only fifty dollars in it. They'd held up the passengers for another fifty.

Fulton had to admit he'd been a little careless when they rode away. The driver had thrown down his pistol, but he'd had himself a shotgun up there, probably under a blanket. He had cut loose with a blast that left a pellet in Fulton's shoulder and several more pellets in one of his men. They had cut their losses and scooted out of there.

Normally, this would have been a good time to lie low in this cabin and let things blow over. The shotgun rider had died, so the men with the badges would be out looking for them for several days. The thing is, Fulton didn't have any money. He was a little too fond of the saloons and gambling houses in Denver to hang on to his cash. His boys needed money, too.

Fulton shifted uncomfortably and watched the flames in the fireplace dying down. Another stage robbery right now seemed like a bad idea. All the stages in this area would have a shotgun rider and a heavily armed driver for a while. That left bank robberies, train robberies, and cattle rustling if they wanted to make some good money. Fulton hadn't been in a train robbery since the night they had hung Ace Musgrove. He didn't plan on another.

Fulton got up, went back over to his mattress, and rolled up in the blankets. He had heard of the idea of rustling cattle and driving the stock to Mexico. They didn't care about brands down there. He hadn't been to Mexico, but he'd heard the cantinas weren't bad. And he knew a guy from his outfit during the war who was interested in buying cows, somewhere around El Paso. That's what he had heard, anyway.

It was a long way to drive some cows, but it would get him and his gang out of the area until things died down. Fulton knew there were some big cattle outfits near Fairplay. As he drifted off to sleep, he decided to scout around for a trail that would at least get them out of Colorado, going south to New Mexico. If they could get to New Mexico, they wouldn't have to do much more than avoid the army. Maybe they could even get all the way to Mexico and sell the cows down there.

I met Sarge early in the morning, and the ride to this place called Lake City only took a day, just like he promised. There wasn't much to see when we got there. What they called the stage stop was more like a livery stable set between a boardinghouse and a café. The stages stopped only about once a week, or so they told me.

The stage that had been robbed had rolled out of town the day before, carrying all the passengers. That left only one person in town who might be able to describe the robbers. They had buried the shotgun rider two days ago, but the driver was still in town. Sarge and I tracked him down in the town café.

He was tying into a giant steak when we got there. He looked friendly enough when he spotted Sarge's badge and waved us into the empty chairs at the table. "Told that sheriff from Gunnison what I know when he come through yestiddy," he mumbled.

I nodded. "We just need a minute," I said, wondering why he was still in town.

"Waitin' for the next stage," he said. I guess he'd read my mind. "Don't got no horse here, so I gotta git the next stage up to Fairplay."

He pushed the steak to the side and waited for our questions.

"You think you hit one of 'em?" I asked.

"Yep. They kilt Jenkins, my shotgun rider. I had my own shotgun under the blanket behind me. When they turned to ride out, I got off a shot. Seen one of 'em lurch a little in the saddle. I'd say I got him for sure. Mebbe got a pellet or two into the guy next to that one."

We talked for a while longer, but he didn't say much that helped. "They rode away to the east," he said, "but they could have circled around when they were out of sight." He couldn't describe anybody. They all wore hats and had bandanas over their faces. He didn't hear any of them say anybody's name.

After twenty minutes, we were out of questions and hadn't learned anything. We left the café and stood outside, looking up and down the street.

"Sorry," Sarge said. "I guess I wasted your time."

I shrugged and crossed the street. "Let's stop in the general store," I said. "Maybe somebody in there can tell us something."

Sarge trailed behind me as we went into the store. The owner waved from behind the counter, looking puzzled when he saw Sarge's badge.

"Don't know anything about the stagecoach robbery," he said. "Can't think of no other reason for a sheriff to come around."

"Didn't think you would," I said, walking over to the counter. "I'm just tryin' to learn a little more about the area. A marshal up in Denver asked me to help out with this stagecoach robbery."

"Okay." He looked even more puzzled.

"Are there any areas outside town here that might make a good hideout for the stage robbers? Someplace they might go an' keep their heads down, maybe take care of wounds? The driver said he could have got some lead into one or two of 'em."

He drummed his fingers on the counter and stared out the window. "Ain't heard of any places," he said. "I've heard talk of places like that up north. South

Park area." He frowned and thought some more. "I guess there could be," he decided, pointing east. "If you git out into them foothills. Can't think why they would hang around here, though. Small town. Got some cattle outfits to the west. Nothin' else around here at all. Quiet place."

That fit everything I was thinking. Nothing about the robbery made any sense. We turned to go, then I thought of something else. "How big are the cattle outfits you said are around here?"

He shrugged. "Not big. Two outfits, mebbe four or five hunnerd head each. They git most of their supplies in here. Bigger outfits are up north, near Fairplay. Sometimes those boys stop off for supplies when they drive some cows down to New Mexico."

That was the first useful thing I'd heard all day, but I couldn't see how it had anything to do with the stagecoach robbery. I exchanged a look with Sarge. "How far out there is the trail they take to New Mexico?"

He looked more puzzled than ever. "Mebbe forty or fifty miles west, I'd say."

"Thanks," I told him. We left and stood outside the store.

"You really think those guys are hidin' out and running an outlaw gang in them mountains?" Sarge asked. He was staring doubtfully off to the east.

"No, I don't think so." I knocked some dust off my hat and put it back on my head where it belonged. "Nothin' makes any sense about that robbery. If there's a gang, it's north of here, I'd say."

We walked back down to get our horses, which we

had left outside the café. "I'll tell Anderson we've got nothin' to go on," I told Sarge. "If there's a gang that wants to rustle some cows and drive 'em south, they'll get closer to Silverton. That's about all we learned today."

The boardinghouse at Lake City wasn't much, but it was either that or the livery stable. Sarge and I bunked in at the boardinghouse, grabbed breakfast as soon as the café opened, then headed home to Silverton. I sent my telegram to Anderson and went home to the ranch. I figured that's the last I would hear about this.

Wes Fulton was a planner. That's what he was counting on to keep from getting strung up like his buddy Ace Musgrove. And that's why he was mad at himself for the botched stagecoach robbery. He hadn't planned it right. His next move needed to bring him some real money. Enough to move out of Colorado and find some fresh ground to plow.

By the time his shotgun wound eased after a couple of days, Fulton had decided on cattle rustling. He'd scouted a few major spreads between Salida and Fairplay already. The Flying W spread, right between the two towns, looked like a good target. He'd figured at least two thousand head out there. The trick would be to get the rustled cows to market for a good sale. That's the part he needed to plan. And he needed to plan it by himself and not share those plans. He trusted nobody.

Now, Fulton was seated at a café across the street from the railroad station in Gunnison, nursing a beer and poring over a railroad map he had just bought. He had no intention of coming back to the station in Gunnison, and that was the point.

When the waitress offered another beer, Fulton just growled, waved her away, and pulled his hat lower. He stared at the map. He had already decided to rustle cows at the Flying W. He had enough men to drive maybe two hundred cows, but how would they get away? That was the real question.

Well, Fulton corrected himself, the real question was: how would he get away and collect the money when they sold the cows? He would split the money four ways if he had to, but he didn't mind losing a man or two along the way.

He traced the railroad lines on the map. They would need to drive the cattle south into the Arkansas River Valley. That was good terrain with grass and water. He wanted to take the cows to Mexico, but he had no intention of doing that on horseback all the way to the border. If he sold around here, too many people would know the Flying W brand.

Making use of the Denver & Rio Grande Railroad, that would be the smart thing to do. He would have to pay off an agent or two at the railroad to look the other way on those Flying W brands, but he was willing to do that. If he could drive those cows a short distance, then take them by rail close to Mexico...

Feeling better about things, he waved for another beer, then went back to his map. The closest place to get the cows to a railhead would be in Salida. He didn't dare go there again, not after that botched stagecoach robbery. He growled again at the thought of that robbery. The waitress dropped his beer glass onto the table and fled.

Fulton went back to his map. His finger traced a line to Durango. He sat back, slurped his beer, and looked at the lines flowing out of Durango. His eyes traveled through a few train stops, then paused at the town of El Paso. A slow smile spread across his face.

Feeling better about things, he bellowed for an apple pie to go with the beer and went back to the train stop at Durango. He didn't intend to ride the train to El Paso along with the rustled cows, but he wouldn't have to. His men could go and hold the cattle there for a few days. He was sure he had a buyer in Mexico. Fulton just needed to lie low for a few days, then get to El Paso on a different train. It was safer for him that way. His buyer from Mexico knew better than to cross him. He intended to walk away from this with a thousand dollars or more in his pocket.

Fulton started tracing the map again at Durango. There was a train from Durango to Silverton. That might work. It was only for passengers and maybe some miners and ore. He'd heard about it—it went through some high passes in the mountains. That's where he could lie low. From there, he could work his way to Denver or back through Durango to get to El Paso.

Satisfied, he folded up the map and stuffed it into his pocket. He had met with his crew an hour earlier, promising them he had a plan and would be back in touch within a few days. They weren't happy about it, but they would wait. First, he decided he needed to take the train to Durango and find an agent who would take his money without checking brands. That man would load the cows without questions. Then Fulton would make the trip to Silverton to find a hideout right away. When he came back through, lying low out there for two or three days should do it.

The waitress was approaching his table with a pot of coffee, but he sent her scurrying back to the kitchen with a glare. He dropped two coins on the table and left without a word, crossing the street back to the train station.

A quick look at the schedule told him he could catch a train to Durango in an hour, then connect through to Silverton later in the afternoon. Fulton bought a ticket, then left to walk down to the livery stable to get his horse. He had the animal loaded into a car for the trip to Durango, then came back into the station and settled down to wait for the next train.

THREE

FLYING W

F ulton settled down in a corner of a saloon he'd found called the *Suds 'n Such*. There were a few rowdy miners slamming down some beers on the other side of the room, but he could ignore them without much trouble. He studied the others in the saloon, much as he had looked over the town of Silverton earlier, before picking this saloon.

Besides the owner handing out drinks behind the bar, there was a guy with a badge perched on a stool and talking to the owner. Fulton took him to be the sheriff in this town. Slim, average height, and maybe in his fifties. He didn't look like your average sheriff, but Fulton watched him for a while longer. He had a feeling he shouldn't overlook this man.

"Kin I getcha anything else?"

Startled, Fulton half-turned in his seat to see who was talking to him. He hadn't seen this guy before. He was tall, wide in the shoulders, and with a tanned face. Fulton looked down to take in the Colt on the man's hip. He looked back up to see a pair of clear, dark eyes studying him. He had a feeling those eyes didn't miss much. Fulton shifted his gaze back to the miners in the other corner before nodding.

"Uh, sure, maybe another beer?"

The man nodded and moved away, then came back with the beer. He left the beer and moved over to join the owner and sheriff at the bar. Fulton sipped at his beer and kept an eye on the new guy. He had the uncomfortable feeling he was being watched. He waved off another beer when the stranger came back to his table.

An hour later, the guy who had brought him the beer left the saloon. He paused at the door to wave to some noisy miners and yelled something about going back to the ranch. Fulton watched through the window as the man mounted and left. Fulton dropped coins on the table and followed. A ranch might be a good hideout when he needed one.

Following from a safe distance as the shadows along the trail lengthened, Fulton pulled up when the man turned off the trail. He watched as the rancher turned his horse into a corral and went into a large stone house.

Staying in the fading light at the side of the trail, Fulton could see a barn and a bunkhouse. He watched as a light flickered and came on in the bunkhouse. His eyes traveled past the barn and out to the surrounding pastures. He could barely make out some foothills rising into the mountains beyond.

Fulton turned his horse and retraced his steps into

town. He had a feeling he could hide out safely up in those foothills. It might come in handy to know that.

Isaiah Washburn had fought tooth and nail for everything he had. He was a veteran of the war and a veteran of two cattle drives on the Goodnight-Loving Trail. He'd saved every penny to drift his own cows along with Goodnight on the last drive, and now he had a spread of almost two thousand head.

That made him feel good and made him feel worried all at once. He had just enough hands to run the place. Folks called him...what was that word they liked to use? Thrifty, that was it. Isaiah was a thrifty man. He liked to say that money stuck to him like burrs on a saddle blanket.

Anyway, he was proud of his spread. What had him worried was the news he had been getting about rustlers striking in Park County, the home county of his precious Flying W ranch. His ranch was on the western side of the county, away from the railhead at Salida. That could help. On the other hand, rustlers could drive his herd south into New Mexico from here. There were good trails along the way.

He hadn't been a victim yet, and he'd only heard of a few cows getting rustled here and there, but he didn't feel like waiting for something big to happen. That's why he had summoned all six of his hands for this meeting. He looked around the barn where they had gathered. Most of these men had been with him for ten years or more. They were the only family he had.

Isaiah cleared his throat and got things started. "I don't know if you've been hearin' what I've been hearin'," he said. "About rustlers, I mean. Rustlers poachin' some cows here and there lately."

He looked around the room. A couple of heads were nodding. "We ain't gonna sit and wait for 'em," Isaiah boomed. "We're gonna be ready and make 'em sorry if they hit the Flying W."

More heads were nodding. They looked at each other and back at Isaiah. "What do you want us to do, boss?" came a question from the side.

The man who'd asked was Abe. Abe was Isaiah's oldest hand, and the truth was, Isaiah had been finding easy jobs for Abe lately. He didn't have the heart to let the man go.

"Extra watches at night, for starters," came his answer. "We've got us some good ground to defend, like they said in the army, so we can make 'em pay. We've got us a valley with some peaks all around. If they hit us, they'll prob'ly drive the cows through Trout Creek Pass at the south."

The heads kept nodding. This was making sense.

"Two extra hands, takin' turns watching the cows every night. That's double the guard we've always had. Now, listen up. I don't want nobody gettin' his fool head shot off if they hit us. You jest fire off yore guns and roust the others of us outta the bedrolls. We all ride for Trout Creek Pass and give 'em a hot reception, all of us together."

They were on their feet now, volunteering for the

extra shifts. Isaiah grinned underneath his bushy mustache. These were good men, ready to fight for the brand. He moved among them, dividing up the extra watch duties. When he had finished, they drifted out for their daily duties. Isaiah then told them he would be gone for the rest of the day.

He moved over to his horse and saddled the gelding for a ride to town in Fairplay. He had one more ace to play about this rustling business.

━━━━

It was a long ride to Fairplay, but this was something he'd been thinking about for a long time. When Isaiah had drifted west after the war, he had tried his hand at mining for a while, settling in the town of Ouray. He'd had no luck finding color, but he had met a lawyer who had come west for his health, and they became friends. That lawyer, Frederick Walter Pitkin, was now the governor of Colorado.

Isaiah dismounted, walked into the telegraph office, and took his time with the message. He told his friend, the governor, he felt sure rustlers were gathering around the South Park area. He asked the governor to send a marshal to look things over. Finally, he promised to gather the leading ranchers in the area to talk to the marshal and give him their support.

Isaiah handed over his message to the clerk and waited until the man finished typing it out. Standing on the boardwalk outside the telegraph office, he tilted his head up at the sun. He estimated he had several more hours before dark. Might as well make the trip worth his while. He headed for a saloon across the street, satisfied that he had done everything he could about cattle rustling for one day.

Frederick Pitkin believed in keeping the peace more than anything else. He wanted a peaceful, quiet state. He smoothed out the telegram from his old friend, Isaiah Washburn, on top of his desk and frowned at it.

Pitkin had worked to settle the feuds between competing railroads and used troops to put down native uprisings and strikes by miners. As a former miner himself, he understood more about mining and railroads than anything else. The citizens demanded protection from Indian attacks, so he didn't hesitate to call out the army when those happened.

Cattle rustling sounded like something he needed to stop. He just wasn't sure how to do that. There were thousands of head of cattle out there on the western slopes. It was a growing industry in the state. His friend, Marshal Brad Anderson, was somebody he would normally call on for something like this, but Anderson had made it clear he was retiring soon.

Pitkin couldn't blame him for that. An outlaw in Leadville had shot Anderson just last year. He had largely recovered, but Anderson's wife and family wanted him at home more and out of the gun sights of Colorado's outlaws.

Still, Pitkin could ask Anderson for advice on this one. How would Anderson stop cattle rustling? There weren't that many marshals in the state, and they were already busy with safeguarding the mining trade and the railroads.

Pitkin pulled out his pocket watch and checked the time, then smiled. He knew exactly where he could find Anderson at this hour. It was lunchtime. If Anderson wasn't still eating lunch, he would probably be talking to friends and colleagues at *Murphy's Exchange*. It was one of Denver's most popular cafés and meeting places. The governor put on his hat and walked down to Murphy's.

Pitkin could see he had arrived just in time. Anderson was standing, draining the last of a glass of beer and reaching for his hat. Pitkin intercepted Anderson on his way out and asked him to join the governor for a talk.

Pitkin was a man who didn't like to waste time talking. He grinned to himself when he thought about that—wasn't that what lawyers were good at, talking? Anyway, he simply passed the telegram from Isaiah Washburn across the table and waited for Anderson to read it.

Anderson read it, reread it, then folded it once and passed it back across the table. "I'm only on the job for another month, Governor. What do you want me to do about this?"

Pitkin spread his hands on the table and waited while a server brought his favorite sandwich.

"I don't expect you to fix this in the month you've got left, Brad, but I need a little advice. Help me understand how to deal with this. Do you think Isaiah could be right? Are we going to have rustling problems in the ranching country?"

Anderson stroked his mustache and nodded slowly. "There's gettin' to be some big herds out there, governor. That means some big money on the hoof. Railroads are spreading out, folks back east and in California will pay for beef..." He nodded again. "Money brings outlaws. We've seen that."

Pitkin nodded unhappily and attacked his sandwich. "Yup. That's kinda what I thought." He shook his head. "There are thousands of acres out there and thousands of cows. How am I supposed to protect 'em all?"

Anderson decided he was still thirsty and waved for another beer. Pitkin waited while Anderson leaned back and slurped at the beer. He pointed at the telegram, now tucked away in Pitkin's pocket.

"One thing, governor, this rancher...Washburn...he said he would get some other ranchers together out there. That's somethin'. They can band together and help each other."

Pitkin brightened a little and went back to his sandwich.

"Two more things, governor," Anderson continued. "We've got militia available if we need 'em, right? We could get 'em out there and ready to go riding on the railroads if we need 'em."

"Done. Tell me who you need."

"Don't need anybody just yet," Anderson answered. "But we had a Captain Hardison and his squad when there was some trouble in Leadville last year. He might be a handy fella to have around."

"Right, Leadville. That's where you got shot, wasn't it? Laid up for a while. You found somebody to come in as a temporary deputy and set things straight. Who was that? Is he still around?"

"Yeah, that's the other thing I wanted to mention. You're talkin' about a friend of mine named Latigo Smith. He don't wanna be a deputy again. He's got him a little ranching spread near Silverton. He might have some ideas, though. Mebbe I could go and see Lat."

Pitkin slapped the table so suddenly that it made Anderson jump in surprise. "I like all those ideas, Anderson," he boomed. "You've got whatever you need." He passed the telegram back across the table. "Can you telegraph Isaiah and ask him to get those ranchers together? Then you can go talk with them."

Pitkin left money on the table for his lunch and Anderson's beer. "Maybe you could stop and talk to this Latigo Smith fella after you see the ranchers. Tell him what's goin' on, at least."

Anderson nodded and watched the governor leave Murphy's Exchange. He would do exactly what the governor asked, with one exception. He would go to see Lat Smith first, even though his gut told him Lat would only get involved if his ranch or family were threatened. Anderson couldn't blame him for that, but maybe he could talk his friend into taking the trip with him to meet the ranchers in South Park.

He left Murphy's Exchange and walked down the street to check on where Captain Hardison and his squad were stationed at present. They had come in handy up there in Leadville.

When I got to the *Suds 'n Such* that night, Holt had a surprise for me. I walked in and saw three miners chugging down their whiskeys and throwing things at the wall. I stopped to watch what they were doing. They were holding little rope circles and throwing them at bottles sticking out of a board.

I stared over at Holt. He just chuckled and kept pouring whiskey over there at the bar. There was a roar from the miners. I looked over and saw a rope circle hanging over a bottle in the middle of the board. Some money changed hands.

I shook my head and went over to the bar. "Well," I mumbled, "we don't allow poker on account it gets too rowdy. I guess this keeps 'em out of trouble." There was another roar when another rope circle landed on a peg.

"How much do they win when they hit a peg?" I asked.

"Five cents for the one in the middle. Two cents for the others. They've been playin' it for hours." He pointed at a freshly emptied bottle of whiskey. "Business is boomin'. Sarge says if they get too rowdy, we can just take the board outside."

I chuckled and settled back to watch. My buddy Dugan was over there, and he couldn't throw a rope circle to save his life, but he made more noise than all of 'em.

Five minutes later, another old friend came through the door. I had the uncomfortable feeling that things were going to change in my life just as soon as I saw him, but I decided to ignore that feeling. Marshal Brad Anderson was a man to ride the river with. We had ridden a few of those rivers already. As I stood up to wave at him, I knew this must have something to do with the stagecoach robbery in Salida, or maybe something new he was worried about.

Holt could see this was gonna be a big pow-wow. He set us up in his office with a pitcher of beer and left us alone to talk. Anderson hoisted his glass and toasted old friends. Now I started to worry, and I couldn't see why we should waste any time getting down to business.

"What's it about, Brad? Another stagecoach robbery?"

His smile faded just a little. He took a big pull at the beer and put it down. "No, there ain't been any more of those." He shook his head. "Stagecoach robberies aren't the guvnor's got me workin' on, anyway."

He reached out with the pitcher to fill up my glass. "You know I'm about to retire from bein' a lawman? Next month!"

This talk wasn't goin' anywhere, but I could see I needed to let him run in circles for a while. Kinda like a stampede. You had to let 'em run till they tired out a little. Then you turned 'em. I just let him talk about what he wanted to do next.

Ten minutes later, he finally got around to it. "Guvnor got a telegram from an old buddy of his, a rancher up in South Park." He passed a wrinkled piece of paper across the desk to me. "Tell me what you think."

I read the telegram and passed it back. "I don't know this Isaiah Washburn," I said. "I've maybe heard of the Flying W spread. I think there's a few folks down here have bought some stock from there."

Anderson leaned forward. "What about the rustling? Have you had any rustling around here?" I shook my head. Anderson frowned. "Any reason you think there could be trouble?"

I shrugged and leaned back. "Outlaws do whatever is working the best and making 'em the most money for the least trouble," I observed. "The Pinks are riding the trains and making train robbing tougher. There's not as many stagecoach riders and not as much money there, unless you rob one carrying ore or payroll."

I took another swallow and thought it over a little more. "If you could poach enough cows and figure how to get out of Colorado with 'em, yeah, there could be some money in that."

Anderson nodded and stood. "That's pretty much what I think. I've been in touch with Washburn, and he's got some other cattle people in the area coming to the Flying W in three days for a meetin'. They want to organize in case there's trouble."

I nodded and waited. That sounded like a good idea. I had a feeling I was about to hear what this had to do with me.

"I was hoping you'd come with me, Lat. You could meet some other ranchers, maybe you would wind up working with them on some things. And I know they'd be glad to hear what you've got to say. Your name carries some weight in Colorado."

I stood up, wondering about leaving the ranch and

family, and wondering what I might be getting myself into.

"Take some time," Anderson said. "Talk to that pretty wife of yours. Meet me in the café in town in the morning? Tell me what you think about it then?"

I agreed to think about it, and I would talk to Joanna. Sometimes it's hard to know if you're getting into something you should stay out of, or if you're just meeting trouble before it gets to your front door.

FOUR
WATCHING AND WAITING

I saiah Washburn pumped my hand and showed me into a big room in the middle of his ranch house. There were six other ranchers I counted there, plus Brad Anderson, who had come up a day ahead of me. I took a seat on the hearth of a big stone fireplace and sipped from a big cup of coffee. I had mostly come to listen to what the others had to say.

There weren't any speeches from anybody, but the ranchers moved around, comparing range conditions, cattle prices, and, of course, rustling activity. I moved around and talked to all of them, thinking this kind of meeting was a good idea. I would have to see if I could get a group like this together down around Silverton.

By the time we took a break for lunch, it seemed like they were all saying the same thing about rustling. Nobody had lost more than a dozen head at any one time, but the attacks were steady. Every week or so, each rancher lost a few cows.

"Almost like they're testing us out, settin' us up for a raid," was the way one guy put it.

All the cows were driven south, as far as anybody had tracked them. All the ranchers were against sending more than one or two hands to track the cows. If they sent more, that would leave the whole herd open for attack back at the ranch. Nobody could spare the extra hands.

There were several trails winding through Colorado and leading south down into New Mexico. Any stolen cows could be driven along any one of the trails, or possibly they could be separated into two or three herds to avoid capture. All the ranchers agreed, though, that any poached cattle would be driven south. There were too many obstacles and much more difficult terrain in the other directions.

Washburn called a break for lunch and served up huge bowls of beef stew and cornbread. His cook was a veteran of a lot of cattle drives and knew how to keep those bowls filled up. I was thinking about looking for a place to take a nap when Anderson came along and asked if I would talk to everybody after lunch.

I frowned. "You mean, make a speech? I hate speeches."

Anderson chuckled. "Yeah, I think we all do. I'm sure you'll keep it short. Just tell these guys what else they can do about the rustlers and ask if there's anything the state of Colorado can do for them. I'll just pass it along to the guvnor."

I just growled a little under my breath, chased

down some more cornbread with a glass of lemonade, and told Anderson I would do it.

It was a little uncomfortable, what with all those faces looking at me and thinkin' I had something more to say than I did, but I told 'em to stick together. I told them to use the telegraph as much as they could. Washburn could check for telegraphs at Fairplay, and the rancher nearest to Salida could do the same there. They could send riders between the ranches to keep each other up on what was happening.

I asked where these rustlers could be hiding. They looked at each other and shrugged. "There's a thousand places up in them foothills," Washburn said. "And they can move to new spots every day. They prob'ly do if they're watching like I think they are. No way to pin 'em down."

I had to agree. I looked around. "Anybody think they can ship out stolen beeves on the railroad?" I asked.

They looked around at each other. "Don't the railroad check for brands?" somebody asked.

"Supposed to," I agreed. "That don't mean a little money couldn't make a railroad agent look the other way." There was a little buzz that went around the room after I said that.

I looked over at Anderson. "We've got the governor's help with this, right? We could have some militia watching the railheads at Salida and Durango. Worth keeping an eye on things." The buzz got a little louder.

"We could use the railroad and some militia to help chase 'em down, too," I said. "Trains can move faster than a herd of cows." I looked over at Anderson again.

"We can have some militia ready to move just as soon as we hear there's been a raid."

Things broke up a little after that, with people talking in small groups. Anderson promised to get in touch with the governor and get Hardison and his squad ready to move. Washburn pulled me aside on my way out.

"Kin I reach you by telegram in Silverton?" he asked. I shuffled my feet a little. I didn't want to get dragged into something so far away from home.

"You can," I agreed, "but I just came to listen and offer any ideas. I'm not the one you'll need. That'll be whoever replaces Anderson."

Washburn just grinned a little. "My old buddy Frederick Pritkin has him a way of talking folks into helpin' where they're needed." He patted my shoulder and walked me to the door.

"You was asking where those scoundrels could be hiding," he said. "There was always stories going around about hideouts in the mountains east of Salida. If I was looking to lay low and set up a job, that's where I'd go."

Washburn came out to the corral with me, where we found Brad Anderson waiting. "Great idea about the railroad," Anderson said. "I'll be in touch with the guvnor and make sure we have some militia ready to roll wherever we want 'em." He stood back while I saddled my horse.

"I might stop by in Silverton before I get back to Denver," he said. "I'm gonna keep you in the picture on this one."

I shook his hand, waved at Isaiah Washburn, and

mounted up. I had done what I'd agreed to do. Time for me to get back to my ranch and my home near Silverton.

Wes Fulton was nestled in a crevice in the foothills above the Flying W spread, well away from the idiots he had recruited to help him pull off this stock poaching. He needed the guns and needed them to be the targets if they should draw any fire, but he didn't want to hear their idiot conversations or complaints about the waiting.

Fulton was going back and forth between two moods today. Those two moods were angry and satisfied. He was happy with the meeting he had set up at the Durango railyards yesterday. It really only took one greedy man to get things rolling, and he'd found a livestock loading supervisor named Tom Steppe at the Durango yards who was definitely greedy enough.

Fulton was pretty tight with his money and didn't really enjoy parting with a twenty-dollar gold piece, but he had to admit it was gonna be quite a bargain after Steppe loaded up his stolen cows and lost the paperwork. Fulton even grinned a little when he thought about that.

The thing that had soured his stomach this morning was all the activity he was seeing down at the Flying W. Tonight was supposed to be the night they struck. Sure, he had seen the extra guard posted last night, but they could handle that. This morning, though, visitors had been coming in all morning. At least eight of 'em he had counted. They had spent hours inside that ranch house.

Now there were three men talking at the corral. He knew the first one. That was the guy who owned this spread. He hadn't seen the other two, so they must be two of today's visitors.

Fulton shifted his position a little and focused the binoculars more closely on the other two. He stiffened when sunlight reflected off a badge. He cursed under his breath and checked the second man. No badge, but that was the guy who'd brought him beer at the saloon in Silverton. What, he wondered, were the chances this guy just shows up at the Flying W for a big meeting?

Fulton set the glasses down and watched as the big guy from Silverton saddled up and left. The one with the badge walked back to the ranch house while the Flying W owner fastened the latch on the corral. Fulton picked up the glasses and focused again, then stiffened when the man down below straightened suddenly and stared up toward Fulton's position.

Fulton gasped, crawled backward, and cursed himself for being seven times a fool. A careless fool, to make things worse. Only one thing could have caused that man to look at his position so suddenly and directly. He'd caught a flash of sunlight off the glasses. Fulton retreated to his horse, mounted, and took off. They would have to delay this for at least another two days. He wasn't looking forward to telling his men.

Things got uglier than expected when Fulton gathered the men. He pulled them back from their positions surrounding the Flying W and refused to answer any questions about the visitors and the meetings going on down there. That part wasn't actually hard to do. He didn't have any answers.

Fulton told them he needed to check things out a little more before they moved. He needed to see if all the visitors had left. He needed to see if they beefed up the night guards even more.

Those things only made sense. The trouble was, these men were broke, tired of living in the hills, and anxious to blow their money from the cattle rustling in a big town. They seemed to have appointed a leader and spokesman for themselves. He was a tall blonde with a hook nose that looked to have been broken a few times. He went by the name of Eli.

Eli had a nasty habit of jabbing his finger in the air to make his point. He was running on now, bellowing about camp food and sleeping in the hills and why couldn't they just take this place down and get outta here?

Fulton refused to back down when Eli moved in on him, jabbing that finger at Fulton's chest. Backing down would be a mistake, Fulton knew that. He moved in, resting his hand on his gun belt. The move wasn't lost on Eli, and he backed off just a tad.

The truth was, Fulton was okay as a gun hand, but he liked to get things in his favor. Things like having bright sunlight in the other man's eyes. Things like getting a buddy to distract his target before they faced off. Fulton had never seen Eli in action and wasn't eager to have a fair fight.

When Eli backed down just a bit, Fulton pressed his advantage and made the peace. He lifted both hands in the air and walked over to his saddlebag. "Okay," he told them, "I know you boys have had to wait. I'm gonna make it up to you."

Reaching into the saddlebag, he pulled a sack from inside and walked around, handing each man a twenty-dollar gold piece. "Two days," he said. "Wait two days before we move. This is yours to keep. Give me two days."

The money had the effect he'd thought. The grumbling melted down to a few halfhearted mumbles, then they all moved off. Fulton kept a neutral expression on his face while he gave Eli his money. He watched Eli move away, mumbling under his breath.

"That one's gonna cost you," he snarled under his breath at Eli's departing back. "I'll get that gold piece outta your pocket when you're dead. That's if you ain't spent it yet."

━━━

It was the idea of an outlaw gang hiding behind a few rocks and trees up in the foothills that just kept sticking in my craw. These gangs were either hiding out in a decent setup somewhere in the mountains or else they were spending all their loot in the nearest town.

I kept thinking about that stagecoach robbery near the middle of nowhere in Salida and what the owner of that general store had said about hideouts off to the east. By the time I got to Washburn's gate, I turned Buck toward the town of Fairplay. The railroad could save me a little time getting home. In the meantime, I wanted to go back and explore a few things in Salida.

A ticket to Salida through Gunnison cost me three dollars. I loaded Buck onto the livestock car and plopped myself down in a seat in the front coach. These narrow-gauge railroad lines were popping up and connecting all over Colorado now. I took some pride in that. I had helped build the first one from Durango to Silverton.

The train pulled out into wide grasslands. I could see how the South Park area was good for cattle ranching. After some time I spent checking the herds and conditions we passed through, the train entered a long tunnel, and I dozed off to sleep. My last thought was about how hard this tunnel would have been for the railroad construction teams. I was glad I hadn't ramrodded this tunnel.

After some good napping and a train switch in Gunnison, we chugged into Salida. Darkness was falling, but I had some time to get over to that general store and see what else the owner could tell me.

He came out from the back when the bell rang to announce me, wiping his hands on a rag and nodding when I started to introduce myself.

"I remember, you and a sheriff come to check on a stagecoach robbery. Ain't been no excitement around here since then." He led the way out front and pointed to a chair for me on the porch. "What kin I do for ya today?"

I decided to put my cards right on the table. "I'm doin' a little checking around for the governor and a state marshal," I told him. "You said something last time about maybe some hideouts up in the mountains and maybe north and east of here. What makes you think so? Where would they be?"

He settled back in his rocker and stared out at the mountains. I jumped when I heard some snoring and turned to see an old guy asleep in a porch swing.

"I jest hear what they say in the store, you understand," he said. He pointed at the guy snoring in the corner. "That's who could tell you more. Old Elmer was around here and up in the South Park area when they first started hitting color. You buy him a dinner over at the diner, and he'll tell you everything he knows an' several things he just thinks he knows. You buy him some apple pie, and he might even draw you a map."

So, five minutes later, Elmer was trotting along beside me to the town diner. When I mentioned apple pie, he even got a pencil and some paper from the general store owner. We settled at a table near the kitchen.

I turned Elmer loose over some fresh trout and stayed out of his way for a while. You don't want to come between a man and his dinner when they're as hungry as Elmer looked.

Finally, he stuffed down the last of his bread, pushed the plate away, and fixed a bleary eye on me.

"Hideout, huh? Mebbe betwixt here and Fairplay, tucked away in the mountains?"

I nodded.

"Hideout for a big crew or a little 'un? How long they gotta stay hid? Some of these places ain't fit for folks when the winter sets in up there."

He had a point there, and I really didn't know. I thought about the small crew they had on the stagecoach robbery. Depending on how big a cattle rustling operation they might be setting up, maybe just a couple more for rustling.

"Small crew," I decided. "Maybe only a couple guys. This time of year, springtime, not too cold up there."

"Yup." He looked around for some apple pie, but I had to get more out of him first.

"You know a place or two? Maybe a day or two's ride from here?"

"Yup. Best hideout I ever laid eyes on. Back when I weren't too partiklar where my money come from. Some say the Reynolds boys used it."

That sounded promising. The Reynolds gang had operated around here after the war. I waited. "How would I get there?"

Elmer belched gently and reached for the paper and pencil. I pushed it over to him.

"You foller the Arkansas River outta town, here, movin' north and east. You'll see a bunch o' mining camps. They might give a man a little dinner if he's hungry." He filled in a few lines on the map he'd started.

"Next, you foller the trail toward Leadville. Ain't

much of a trail, jest a few rutted tracks. You can see it, though. You go along a few miles and then set yore sights on Mosquito Pass. Highest thang around. You cain't much miss it."

His eyes lit up when the apple pie arrived. He took his time on that pie, but I wasn't going anywhere tonight. Finally, he reached for the pencil and paper again.

"There's a long, narrow gorge windin' along toward that pass. Don't much know how to tell you to find it, but if'n you get down into that gorge and keep them eyes peeled, there's a cabin set against the side of a cliff. There's a cave behind the cabin. Best hideout I ever seen. A few guys could stay lost back there for a while."

He pushed the empty plate to the side, laid down the pencil, and dozed off to sleep over the table. I gently pulled the map from under him, studied it, then sighed and tucked it into my pocket. There wasn't much chance I could find this place unless I was following somebody, but maybe it would come in handy someday.

I left some money on the table and left Elmer sleeping off his dinner. It was a boardinghouse for me tonight, and then I would be on the trail for Silverton early tomorrow.

———

Isaiah Washburn kicked at the embers where the campfire had been, muttering to himself and looking up every now and then to see his Flying W spread below. Somebody had been watching, that was for sure. He hadn't imagined that flash of sun reflecting off glass or metal.

He walked in a circle around the fire, looking for tracks. He found nothing to help him. Returning to the campsite, he kicked dirt over the embers and moved back to his horse. There was nothing more he could do. He was sure the rustlers would come.

FIVE
SOUTH TO THE RAILS

Wes Fulton was sure he had set this raid up just as well as he could. He and his three men were poised and waiting in between Buffalo Peaks on his right and the Mosquito Range on his left. Trout Creek Pass lay before them, and the sun was just coming up, showing the way out of this valley. They could drive at least a hundred head of cattle right through that pass and keep them going south.

The trouble was, Fulton was sure the guard had been doubled down there on that Flying W spread a few days ago. Just a few hours ago, he had personally found and taken out one hand when he'd slipped up on the guy dozing in the saddle. A reverse-grip blow from Fulton's Colt had taken care of him. The other guard, though, was nowhere to be seen, if in fact there really was another guard.

Fulton and his men were guessing the herd below had about one hundred fifty head of cattle. They wouldn't get all of them, but they would take enough to make this raid worth their while. Each man carried a covered, trimmed lantern, but Fulton was guessing they wouldn't need them. The sun would be up in just a few minutes.

Fulton edged his horse forward, watching as his men spread out on either side of him. The morning dawn was just touching the wildflowers in the meadow, making the light just right to strike and drive this herd through the pass.

It was quiet. That was bothering Fulton. He didn't hear the hands singing to the herd. He didn't hear any elk bugling, and he didn't hear coyotes yipping. The wild animals were aware of Fulton's crew, making the sunrise a silent one. Were the Flying W hands aware, too? Could this be a trap?

If he called off the raid now, he would pretty much have a mutiny on his hands. He had stalled these boys as long as he could. Fulton leaned forward and got ready to launch a loud *yip* to get the cows moving. The noise never left his lips.

A shadow came up from the brush in front of him. Fulton could see just well enough to see a rifle coming level. There was a shout, followed by a loud crash from the rifle. One of Fulton's men corkscrewed side-ways and fell from the saddle.

It was pure instinct to pull his Colt and drop the man in front of him. The cattle bawled and surged forward. "Let 'em go," Fulton yelled. Nobody had to tell the men to leave their man who had been shot from the saddle. They spread out and chased the stampeding herd toward Trout Creek Pass, urging them on with cracks of their whips.

Fulton glanced nervously toward his left, toward the ranch buildings. The gunshots would alert everybody on the property. A light came on in the big stone house now, and a rifle shot whined over his head. Men were scrambling from the bunkhouse and toward the corral. Fulton pressed himself flat against the saddle and urged his horse on. None of them bothered to return fire. There was almost no chance of hitting anything other than each other.

Some of the herd leaders began drifting to the sides, but that was good. There was a narrow, rocky ravine leading into Trout Creek Pass, and the entire herd wouldn't fit into that ravine, especially not when they were moving at this speed.

The gunshots were coming from behind them now as the ranch hands mounted to give chase, but it was scattered fire. His men all had dark ponchos wrapped around themselves, and leaning over the saddles, they presented very small targets.

Fulton estimated they had eighty or ninety cows in front of them when the herd hit the rocky ravine and slowed. Fulton and his crew yipped and snapped whips in the air to keep them moving as they pressed from behind.

Emerging from the rocky draw, the cattle began climbing the ascent through Trout Creek Pass. "Keep 'em going," Fulton yelled, waving his hat. "Down into the Arkansas River Valley." He reined in and dropped behind a boulder at the side of the path leading up and through the pass.

"I'm gonna keep 'em off our backs," he yelled. "When they reach the river, let 'em stop."

Fulton pulled his Winchester from the scabbard and laid it across the top of a boulder. The Flying W hands appeared in the ravine below, moving slowly, but still coming on.

Fulton laid his sights on the front rider's chest, then raised the sights by two feet. The first shot would be a warning, but there would be only one warning. All five riders skidded to a stop when the shot rang out. They circled, then retreated.

Satisfied, Fulton remounted his horse and turned to catch up to his gang and the stolen cows. They would keep a steady pace all the way to the rail yard at Durango, then ship the herd to El Paso. Nobody would catch them now.

He reached the others before they came to the Arkansas River Valley. He found them pulled up at an overlook. The ribbon of the river wound through the fields below. Below the river, they could see the pale green of the San Luis Valley, stretching away from them toward the south.

Fulton confirmed what he'd thought when one of his men went down back there at the Flying W. It was Eli, the troublemaker, who'd been killed by the rifle shot. Fulton couldn't have planned it any better.

Isaiah Washburn reined in and commanded his men to back off just as soon as a bullet ricocheted off the cliff face behind him. They were sitting ducks for somebody who was parked up there with a Winchester right now. Maybe his shot had missed on purpose and maybe it hadn't.

Washburn's men regrouped behind a nest of boulders, but Washburn knew they couldn't stay here for long. A few shots off the granite walls behind them would make it far too hot to stay hidden where they were.

Feeling rage and frustration, Washburn looked around him. Two men were missing—the two men who had taken the watch tonight. One was a young, red-cheeked boy named Zeke, and the other was his oldest hand, Abe. A sick fear rose in his throat as he ordered his men to return to the Flying W and search for the missing hands.

When they retraced their path, they found the ground at the ranch had been torn up and trampled by the stampede. Following the trail of the stampede from Trout Creek Pass back to where it started had been easy. They all called out the names of the missing men as they rode, hoping for an answering shout.

Washburn was the first to see the bundle on the ground just past the place where the stampede had started. The bundle was twisted in an odd way, and Washburn was pretty sure what he would see. He dismounted and knelt beside the corpse. It was Abe. Washburn stood and turned away, fighting the urge to retch while the others continued the search for Zeke.

The only good news of the day came a few minutes later, and another five minutes past the starting point of the stampede. They heard a voice calling from behind a stand of sagebrush. It was Zeke, the kid. He was tied hand and foot and had a large knot on the back of his head, but he was otherwise unharmed.

Unfortunately, Zeke could remember almost nothing. The world had blacked out and he'd come awake, tied up as they found him. Isaiah was pretty sure the kid had drifted off to sleep in the saddle and got knocked on his head. No matter now, the damage was done.

Washburn made the trip to Fairplay that afternoon and sent another telegram to his friend, the governor.

━━━

Brad Anderson walked Captain Hardison and his ten Colorado militiamen down to the train station and briefed Hardison while the men waited to board the train. News of the raid at the Flying W had come through yesterday, and Anderson had lost no time getting the governor's permission to call out the militia.

Isaiah Washburn estimated the rustlers had gotten away with about ninety head of cattle. All had the Flying W brand. Washburn estimated that even if they moved the herd late into the night all the way, they would need ten days to get to Durango.

"You boys are going through Pueblo, then on a narrow-gauge rail west," Anderson explained. "It's gonna take you the better part of two days, but you'll have a jump on the rustlers if they're going to Durango."

Hardison nodded silently, deciding on whether he should ask the question in his mind.

"I know, what if they didn't go to the railroad at Durango?" Anderson prompted. Hardison nodded again, relieved he hadn't had to ask that one.

"Yeah, that's the hard part," Anderson agreed. "They almost had to go south to find a market and have terrain they can drive a herd through. Maybe they could go over to the rails at Salida, but a herd that big would draw a lot of attention in Salida."

Anderson paused and thumped his fist on the seat while he thought. "I might take a train to Salida myself and see what I can see."

The train pulled in and the militiamen stood, waiting to board. Anderson filled in his final thoughts. "If they take trails south through New Mexico, we'll probably have to ask the army to help. In any case," he finished, "let me know by telegraph if you get there and haven't found any trace of the rustlers and cows within maybe ten days. Send the telegram to me here in Denver." He thought a second longer. "Send the same telegram to Latigo Smith in Silverton. He might have some other ideas on what we can do."

Anderson stepped back while the locomotive belched and poured smoke, then the train slowly pulled away from the station. He had a few other cases to work on for the next few days. After that, what he did depended on what Hardison and his men could find in Durango.

Wes Fulton had never been on a cattle drive. He had a map showing the trails he could follow and marking the water sources, so at least he knew the route. His men were happy enough to shoot the food they needed, but nobody showed much interest in cooking it. They wound up living on coffee and some jerky he'd bought along when they ate breakfast. Dinnertimes, they drew straws for who would cook. Venison they shot and some beans they stopped to buy along the way were on the menu every night.

After a few days on the trail, Fulton relaxed a little. They came down from the nine-thousand-foot elevation where they had started, moving toward the San Luis Valley. Nights were still cold but not freezing. They passed only the occasional traveler on this remote trail, and nobody challenged them.

Worried about meeting his buyer on time in El Paso, Fulton began pushing the crew and cattle to move a little farther each day, driving farther south each night under the moonlight.

It was on the fourth night of the trip that Fulton found out what could happen when the thunderstorms blew in off the mountain. It was well past sundown on this night, and Fulton was scouting a place to stop for the night when the wind picked up.

Satisfied with the meadow he'd found, Fulton was moving back to the herd when jagged streaks of lightning flickered off to the north. He picked up the pace and had just spotted the herd when the wind stiffened sharply, and a low growl of thunder sounded.

A low grumbling, bawling noise sounded from the cattle as the thunder picked up in intensity. An ear-splitting clap of thunder and a bolt of lightning touching down behind the herd was all it took. Fulton barely had time to process the sight of the entire herd bearing down on him, horns flashing in the flickers of lightning.

Frozen for an instant by the bellow of the cattle and the feel of the ground shaking, Fulton reacted just in time, turning his gelding and raking his spurs across the animal's ribs.

Outrunning them was a terrifying idea and maybe not possible. Fulton angled the horse across the meadow, banking on outracing them to the edge of the field before he was trampled. As he neared safety, he could see the wild eyes in the moonlight and sense the incredible power of the onrushing herd.

When he reached the edge, and the herd swept past, Fulton kept the horse running. He didn't need one stray at the edge of the herd colliding with them after he thought they were out of the way. Finally, when all the cattle had passed, he reined in and stared as they careened away from him.

Fulton passed the back of his hand across his forehead and cursed bitterly. There was no telling where the herd would stop, and how many of them they could recover and drive to Durango. He stared off to the north. With the lightning dying away, it was hard to see how many of his crew had survived this.

With another glare toward his disappearing herd, Fulton reined his horse around and went to see if his hands had survived.

The crew survived because nobody had been riding point. That was Fulton's job, and he had been far enough in front to escape the herd. Fulton used threats to keep them riding forward to look for the herd. When that didn't work, he reminded them nobody would be paid if they didn't have any cows to deliver in Durango.

The South Arkansas River was what had saved Fulton's herd from scattering. They had been two days without water, and when the thunderstorm died away, they stopped at the river's edge to drink.

Fulton and his crew found them there at mid-morning the next day, grazing, drinking, or simply lying down at the river's edge. Fulton called a halt to water the horses and find some food for the crew. Moving on at dawn the next morning, they reached the edge of Durango just one week later.

━━━

Fulton rode ahead to Durango. The cattle stayed in a valley three miles north of town, held there by his three trail hands. A ride along Main Street showed a bustling town around him. The railroad had brought a lot of business to Durango.

It was the strong presence of the militia in town that bothered Fulton. He had counted eleven men in uniform, patrolling the streets and paying particular attention to the railroad station and yards around it. There was also a sheriff for the county with an office in Durango, along with the sheriff's deputy. That looked like a lot of badges for a town with not much more than a thousand people, in Fulton's opinion.

Even getting in touch with Steppe, the railroad guy he'd paid to ship the cows, was making Fulton jumpy. Getting close to Steppe at the rail yards brought him closer to the militia patrolling the place.

Fulton watched the station and waited for Steppe to leave the railroad station. The guy had to eat some-time, didn't he? His patience paid off a little after one o'clock when Steppe left the rail yards and headed for a diner on Main Street. Fulton waited until Steppe went in and was seated, then he slipped in and took a seat opposite Steppe.

Steppe looked up in surprise. His jaw dropped a little when he recognized Fulton. "What're you...?"

Fulton kept his head down, growling at Steppe to shut up and go back to looking at the menu. Steppe did so after a moment, but the surprise still showed on his face. Fulton, glancing sideways, saw a militia captain who seemed to be watching. Maybe, he thought, this hadn't been a good idea, either.

Blocking his mouth with his menu, Fulton kept it short. "Cows are just outside of town," he mumbled. "My boys will bring 'em in tomorrow mornin'. Just ship 'em to El Paso, to the guy I told you about before."

Steppe shook his head, glancing over toward the militia captain. He waited while a waitress came to take their orders.

"Too many badges and uniforms around town," Steppe hissed. "Place is crawlin' with 'em. All over the yards down there at the station, they are. Them's some rustled stock yore bringin' me, for sure."

Fulton felt a flush of anger rising in his cheeks and waited while he calmed down. "What'd you think I paid you for? You done got your money, now ship the cows. What do you care? All you're doin' is shippin' animals like you always do."

"Didn't get paid enough," Steppe insisted. "I'll bet those cows of your'n got themselves a brand folks around here would know. I ain't getting paid to ship rustled cows an' git my neck stretched. And I didn't get near enough from you to risk my neck."

Fulton waited, calming himself down again. This was about money, like he'd guessed. Well, Steppe had him hog-tied on this one. Fulton had brought those cows all this way, but he still had to get his money.

Fulton sighed and reached into his pocket. Making sure the militia captain was looking the other way, he slid a twenty-dollar coin across the table. Steppe covered it in a second and slipped it into his pocket.

"Still not enough," he hissed.

Fulton glared, but Steppe wasn't backing down. Fulton slid another twenty across the table. Steppe pocketed that one too, and they ate lunch in total silence.

A few tables away, Captain Hardison finished his lunch and left a few coins on the table to pay for it. He'd been watching the railroad agent for a few days and hadn't seen anything unusual until just now.

Hardison stepped outside and put on his hat. He would tell his men to watch Steppe from a distance but stay alert for any herds up to one hundred head coming to the railroad. Meanwhile, he would follow the other man he had seen in the diner. His gut told him he had just found the rustler they were looking for.

SIX

ESCAPE FROM DURANGO

C aptain Hardison kept his instructions simple because he expected a rustled herd to come from the north side of town. That narrowed down what they were looking for. He had seen the stranger yesterday, leaving the café in that direction before he'd holed up at a boardinghouse. The militiamen were to let the cattle proceed to the rail yards and be placed in the pens. When one of the rustlers met with a railroad agent and paid for passage, they were to step in and arrest everyone.

It almost worked out that well. Five minutes after the railroad agent, Steppe, and all the hands driving the Flying W cattle were arrested, there was just one man missing. Hardison checked and rechecked the men they had arrested. The stranger from the meeting at the café yesterday wasn't here. Hardison had followed the man after leaving the café, but that trail seemed to lead nowhere. The man had disappeared into a boardinghouse and stayed there for at least an hour.

Now, Hardison walked along the lineup of arrested men and stopped at Steppe, the loading supervisor. "Where's the man you had lunch with at the diner yesterday?" he asked softly.

Steppe stared off into the distance. "Dunno what you're talkin' about," Steppe answered defiantly.

Hardison turned to one of his men. "Get me the stationmaster." The militiaman disappeared into the station and came back with a man carrying some papers and wearing a pair of glasses perched on the bridge of his nose.

"Stationmaster Jones, sir! Captain Hardison!" The militiaman Hardison sent snapped off a salute, along with his introduction.

Jones looked from Hardison to Steppe, confusion clear on his face. "What seems to be the problem, Captain?"

Hardison wasted no time. "Your man here is getting ready to load stolen cattle, Mr. Jones. He has about eighty head of cattle belonging to the Flying W Ranch in South Park. I observed him accepting payment for shipping."

Jones's Adam's apple bobbed up and down several times while he stared at Agent Steppe. "I'm sure there's a misunderstanding, Captain. Steppe, do you have a bill of lading or a letter from the Flying W?"

Steppe stared at the ground and shook his head, spreading his hands to show he had nothing. Hardison stepped back in front of Steppe and leaned in.

"His name. I need to know his name. Who talked to you about loading these cows?"

Steppe shook his head. "He didn't give me no name. He come around here a couple weeks ago and paid me to ship these cows to El Paso without no questions asked. He come back yestiddy and paid me a little more."

Hardison shook his head in frustration and rocked back and forth on his heels. The trouble was, he had a feeling Steppe had already told him everything he knew. The man behind the rustling had probably slipped away.

Finally, he turned to an officer. "Take these men to the sheriff in town and tell him to hold them until I can get orders from Marshal Anderson." He turned to Stationmaster Jones. "You're to hold these cattle in these pens until you receive news from Isaiah Washburn of the Flying W Ranch on when he will come to get them."

Stationmaster Jones bobbed his head twice and shuffled away.

When he was left with just his remaining men, Hardison gave orders to two men to guard the cattle, with instructions to the others that they change shifts every four hours.

Hardison walked back into town and over to the telegraph office. He sent two messages. One he sent to Marshal Anderson, saying he had recovered the cattle. The second went to Isaiah Washburn at Fairplay, telling him to come and get his cows.

━━ ━━

Fulton had joined his men for the drive into the Durango rail yards, but he never had any intention of being with them when they handed the cattle over. He took the drag position on the way into town and, half a mile away from Durango, stopped to examine his horse's hooves. He waved the other rustlers away.

"Take 'em on in," he barked. "Give 'em to an agent named Steppe! He'll know what to do."

Fulton waited while they disappeared around a bend, then followed slowly, alert for any militia watching the herd. Seeing none, he followed the herd until he reached a small rise outside of town. He dismounted, laid down at the top of the rise, and waited to see what would happen.

Fulton was stunned when his men were arrested immediately. Militiamen came from everywhere the second the cattle were secured. He watched while all three of his men and Steppe were marched away in handcuffs.

Fulton crawled back from the rise, too stunned to swear. That would come later. He squatted on his heels at the bottom of the rise and thought. There were still militiamen all over town. The sooner he could get away, the better. He crawled to the top of the rise again and swept the area with his binoculars. Only two militiamen were left, and they were guarding the cattle. The others seemed to have gone into town.

It was time to get a ticket to Silverton. He didn't know what to do when he got there, but he wasn't going to El Paso now. He had no cows to sell. He could lie low in Silverton and think of a way to get some money, or he could get back to his cabin hideout near

Salida. He had a few dollars stashed up there for times like this.

Fulton cursed all the way to town, then stalked into the railway station. Finally, he found that he had a little luck on his side. There was a train leaving for Silverton in two hours. Fulton bought a ticket and sat at the side of the waiting room, hat pulled low. Getting out of Durango was the first thing to do.

The two hours crawled past. When the militia captain from yesterday passed by outside, he lowered his head and pulled his hat as low as he could. He was the first one out the door and onto the train when they boarded for Silverton.

━━━

Marshal Anderson read Hardison's telegram about the arrests in Durango as a smile spread across his face. He stayed at the telegraph office for a few more minutes as he sent a few telegrams of his own.

The first one went to the governor, telling him about the recovery of the cattle and the arrest of the rustlers. He had a feeling the governor would be in touch with the newspapers shortly after getting this good news.

He sent his next telegram to Captain Hardison, offering congratulations and giving further instructions. That was about the time he had a few puzzling questions that popped up in his brain.

The cattle were to be loaded onto a trail going to El Paso. The crooked railway agent had told them that much. Who was buying these cows? For that matter, who was selling these cows? It sounded like Hardison had maybe caught a few hired hands, but who was really behind this thing?

After a few more minutes of thinking, Anderson decided he wanted to talk to Hardison in person. Where to meet, that was the question. Anderson himself was in Salida, Hardison in Durango.

He pictured the Colorado rail lines in his head for a minute, then sent the telegram, directing Hardison and his men to meet him in Silverton. He sent a third telegram to Latigo Smith before leaving the telegraph office.

Arriving in Silverton, Wes Fulton headed straight for a boardinghouse, stopping at a saloon only long enough to get himself a bottle of whiskey. He lowered it by half within an hour after checking into a room at a hotel.

His plan was shot to pieces. There were militia guarding the cows, and his men had all been arrested. That part didn't really bother him much, but the cows would go back to the Flying W, and he was too smart to strike in that area again this soon. Besides, he didn't have a crew anymore. He had no money in his pockets for any of his troubles. He went back to the whiskey bottle until he fell asleep.

Morning found him in bad shape. His temple throbbed and he felt like his tongue had grown hair. It took a minute to even remember where he was. He moaned when he remembered. He was stuck in the town of Silverton with no money. Fulton decided on a train to Salida and a trip to his hideout to get the money he had stashed there.

Breakfast at a diner improved his mood very little. The coffee scalded his tongue and throat when he gulped it. His stomach protested at every bite he swallowed. He stood, threw a little money on the table, and stalked outside.

One look at the overhead sun told him the railway office should be open. He would get that ticket to start him on the road to Salida. Just getting out of this town, that was the important thing. Looking both ways, he spotted the rail station and started for it.

A second later, he froze in his tracks. There was a squad of militia stepping down from a train. He shook his head, then clamped his hands to his temples and swore profusely until the pounding let up. These were the same militiamen he had seen in Durango! He was sure of it.

While he watched, he saw two more people he had watched through his glasses recently. He had seen both at the Flying W Ranch in South Park. One was a marshal. The other was a guy he had seen both at the Flying W and at the *Suds 'n Such* saloon here in Silverton. He hadn't liked what he'd seen of that guy either time. He didn't like what he saw now any better. This guy could be trouble.

Fulton whirled and stopped just short of running into a guy standing behind him. The man cursed and gave him a shove. Fulton staggered, regained his balance, and struggled to focus his eyes. He looked at the stranger and decided to walk away. The man was tall with dark hair, wide shoulders, and a deep scar running down his entire left cheek.

Fulton swerved around the man and trotted back to his hotel room. He slammed the door shut behind him and slumped into a chair. This changed everything. With the militia and a marshal down there at the train station, he wasn't going to try getting to Salida right now. He had his horse, but he didn't plan to smack the back of a horse through these mountains. The best way to get to Salida from Silverton was by the narrow-gauge railroads.

He'd done his work on the routes. There was a train from Silverton to Alamosa, then another from Alamosa to Salida. That was the easiest way to go. Mountain passes were hard to cross on horseback, even at this time of year.

The biggest problem was that the train station was swarming with militia and lawmen. Fulton needed to get out of town until things settled down.

That was when he remembered the ranch he had scouted before on his trip to Silverton. Back then, his plan was to hide out there, then go down to El Paso to sell the cows. Now he just needed to hide for a few days. Maybe then he could get to Salida.

Matt Warner had been watching Silverton for two days now. Actually, he had been watching the Silverton Bank for two days. He kept moving around the town, but he always came back to the bank. The scar on his cheek made him more noticeable, so he tried to keep moving and not be too obvious while he studied the bank and the town.

He had decided that he and his two partners, Tom and Bryce Castle, might want to pay this bank a visit. It might work out just as well as their robbery of a bank in Telluride last year.

They took pride in setting things up just right ahead of time. Warner was really the gun hand and enforcer for the gang, but he liked to check things out ahead of time, too. He'd seen how that could pay off.

Warner was here to look at the bank, of course. He'd gone inside just long enough to get the layout, and he had watched the stream of customers going in and out. There were a lot of miners and a few ranchers around here. All of them were likely to have some money they were leaving in that bank.

Besides the bank, he was watching the town. There was a sheriff. He might be a little trouble, but not too much, in his judgment. The town was pretty busy in the mornings and afternoons, but it quieted down around noon. That would be the time to hit the bank.

Studying the bank one more time, he got the uncomfortable feeling he was being watched. He shifted his gaze and started moving away immediately. There was a squad of militiamen and a marshal over there, along with another guy. It was the other guy who was studying him. Tall, broad shoulders, dark hair, black hat, penetrating gaze, just watching him.

Matt Warner turned and moved to check out of his hotel. Time to get out of town. He would remember it, though, and suggest it to Bryce and Tom Castle. This looked like a good possibility.

━━━

I took Anderson, Hardison, and the militia boys down to the *Suds 'n Such*. Holt only griped for a while when I told him the house was paying for the free round of beer. The militia boys only whined for a while after I told them that only the first round was free.

Hardison told us what had happened with the arrest of the rustlers in Durango. Anderson had questions about the prisoners. Hardison had questioned them, but they'd given him few answers. Steppe, the corrupt railway agent, didn't seem to know anything beyond what he'd been told about shipping the cows to El Paso.

It was when Hardison told us about the two men talking in the café at Durango that things seemed to take shape in my head. Hardison's guess was probably right. The man who had been behind this entire operation had stayed back and let everybody else get arrested. There had to be somebody else out there we had missed. It was likely to be the man Hardison had followed from the café in Durango.

Anderson agreed with me. Hardison said he'd had a hunch that the other guy at the café was involved with this, but he couldn't give us much of a description. Average height and weight, sandy-colored hair and beard. That could have been a lot of guys.

All of that left us trying to decide what to do next. Isaiah Washburn was sending a few men to get his cows back from the rail yards at Durango, and the governor was happy for now.

We decided to split up and go three different ways. My job in this was mostly to advise Anderson and help keep the governor happy. I could do that from home in Silverton. I was staying here and hoping that would be the end of it.

Anderson decided to take the train down to El Paso with just one of Hardison's militia boys and look for any cattle buyers who didn't seem too particular about what brand the cows were wearing.

Hardison would take the rest of his militia back up to the South Park area and keep an eye on things for a while. He would check in with Washburn and the other ranchers to see if they were having any more rustling problems. We broke up the meeting and went our separate ways. I saw them all out at the door, then went to help Holt behind the bar for a while.

It was late afternoon by the time I left the *Suds 'n Such* and headed out for my ranch. I moved Buck along at a steady trot, checking the pastures we passed by and keeping a weather eye on the clouds above us.

We were only a mile or two from the ranch when I first noticed the fresh tracks on this trail. We'd had a spatter or two of rain this afternoon, so I knew the tracks were fresh, and whoever had left them was moving toward the ranch.

It was when the tracks left the trail and cut across my western pasture that the hairs on the back of my neck went up. Anybody with friendly intent, even if I didn't know 'em, would just ride up and hello the house. Who cuts across a pasture that goes nowhere except into the foothills?

I moved Buck into the pasture and followed the tracks for a while. This guy wasn't wandering around —he was headed straight up into the foothills. I pulled up and squinted up into those foothills. If an unfriendly face was up there right now, I could be in his crosshairs at his very moment. Plus, the light would be fading soon. Time to move out.

I turned Buck around and headed for the house. First thing in the morning, I would be varmint huntin' up in those hills.

Fulton got himself settled in, dragging his bedroll under the hollow left by a fallen cedar tree. He staked out his horse and gave him some grub, then fished around in his saddlebag for some jerky.

He stood near his horse, letting his eyes rove over the pasture below him, then came to attention when he saw movement down there. Somebody was tracking him! Fulton went to his saddlebag again and pulled out his binoculars. He watched while the man stopped, stared up into the hills, then turned around and went back to the trail and moved out.

Fulton stowed the glasses and swore to himself while he chewed the last of the jerky and swallowed it. It was too late to move tonight, but he knew he needed to be out of here at first light.

SEVEN
TRAIL TO SALIDA

F irst light didn't come soon enough for Wes
Fulton. He tossed in his bedroll, worrying about
the man who had been trailing him across the pasture.
His men had been arrested, and the law might have
made the connection on Fulton's role in the rustling. It
was his plan, after all. What if somebody had talked to
that marshal?

It was the full moon that convinced him to leave
during the night. There was plenty of light to retrace
his steps down that trail to Silverton. He scrambled
out of his bedroll, and in fifteen minutes, he had
loaded his gear and saddled up. He led his horse
down a narrow trail to the pasture below and rode to
Silverton.

Fulton dismounted a few minutes outside of town
and led his horse off the trail and out of sight as the
gray dawn light slowly lit up the town. He waited a
while longer until the street showed signs of activity,

with shopkeepers opening doors and the occasional wagon rolling past him.

Moving directly to the train station, he stepped to the window, tugging at his hat as he asked about the train to Alamosa. He was in luck—there was one train daily, leaving this station in one hour. Fulton bought his ticket. He arranged to have his horse loaded, then he sat in a corner of the room, ignoring the growls from his stomach. He couldn't afford to show himself in the café.

When the train was called, Fulton waited for everyone else to board, then swung into the last car just as the train pulled away. He watched for activity at the station, but no one was running to catch the train. He finally allowed himself to relax as they gained speed and pulled away from Silverton.

My plan was to slip away at daybreak to scout those tracks and check for anybody hiding in the foothills above the ranch. With a little luck, I thought I could be back by breakfast time without worrying Joanna. I should have known it wouldn't work.

Her question stopped me just as I was easing through the back door in our kitchen. "What is it?"

I stopped and turned, resting the butt of my Winchester on the floor. "I saw tracks last night. Recent tracks, headin' up into the foothills above the west pasture. Got too dark to follow 'em. I need to check those out."

I paused, watching her face. She knew me too well,

so I needed to tell her what really bothered me. "What with the cattle rustling up north, and they didn't catch the guy runnin' that show, at least it didn't sound like they did…well, I can't rest easy without scoutin' around up there."

She nodded and crossed the kitchen to give me a kiss. "Be careful and take Otis with you."

She had a point there. Otis was likely up already, and he could cover my back. I found him sitting on the porch at the bunkhouse, sipping at some coffee. Otis called it coffee, anyway. I'd had some and still couldn't identify what was in there. He stood when he saw me coming.

"What's the trouble, boss?"

I explained, and he trotted behind me to the corral. We moved out, heading directly north to the foothills. I wanted to come at this guy from the side, not frame ourselves to get shot at if we rode in directly from that western pasture.

It took only fifteen minutes to reach the tracks leading up to the foothills, and my heart sank as soon as I saw them. There were two sets of tracks now! One led up and the other led back down. In another ten minutes, we had checked the spot where he'd bedded down and followed the outgoing tracks back to the trail to Silverton.

I parted ways with Otis at the corral and told him to keep an eye on the place. Returning to the house, I found Joanna and Ethan having some breakfast in the kitchen.

"Da!"

Ethan thought it was playtime. I had to disappoint

him on that. I reluctantly explained to Joanna that this guy had gotten away. I suspected he had taken a train out of town. She agreed I needed to check it out and saw me out the door.

When I reached Silverton, I went straight to the train station, following my hunch. I talked to the clerk selling tickets. A train had left for Alamosa just about an hour ago. The picture flashed through my head from Hardison's description of an average-weight, average-height guy with sandy-colored hair he'd seen at the café in Durango.

The clerk nodded immediately. "Yep. A guy like that caught the train for Alamosa this mornin'. He sat over there and didn't move a muscle till the train come through. Kept his hat way down, didn't look at nobody."

The clerk filled in a few details. The guy was wearing a red-checked shirt and a long black duster coat. He had a white hat that he kept pulled down all the time. I thanked the clerk and went back out to mount up.

I stopped off at the café and gave them the description of this guy, just to see if he had stopped in. They all shook their heads. He hadn't been here this morning. I moved out to the porch to think things over. He had come to Silverton at the crack of dawn just to get out of town.

These guys tended to work the same towns and counties. That's what I had mostly seen, anyway.

Sometimes a gang would keep moving, hitting new towns, but a lot of times they worked the same area, going from rustling to bank robberies to train robberies. They moved on when the law caught up to them.

This guy was working central Colorado. And his area now included Silverton and my ranch. I couldn't let that ride. I mounted Buck and turned him toward home.

I shook my head when I thought about things on the way back to the ranch. I was going to have to follow this guy. He fit the description of the head rustler, and he had been hiding out at my ranch. I couldn't let this one go. I sighed when I thought about explaining this to Joanna and how I would have to hit the trail soon to track this guy.

The train let out a whistle and belched smoke into the air as we pulled out of Silverton. The streets were busy with freight wagons and with miners riding into town to spend some of their hard-won gold and silver ore. Silverton was a bustling little town, and I was proud of it.

We wound along the path of the Animas River, heading for the cliffs, trestles, and narrow passages in the San Juan Mountains. It seemed like ten years ago I had worked to help build these railroad tracks. In fact, it had been only two.

I leaned back in my seat and thought about the scene around my dining room table just last night.

Ethan was asleep in the bedroom. Joanna sat by my side. Otis, Holt, and Sarge were gathered around the table along with Dugan, the giant redheaded miner.

I knew I had to track this man. We were all convinced he was a part of, and probably the leader of, the rustling operations up in South Park. No one knew how he had become connected to Silverton and to my ranch, but I knew we had to meet trouble head-on.

They all knew I would be on today's train to Alamosa. The meeting last night was to decide how to protect the town of Silverton and my ranch and family. Joanna was mighty handy with a Winchester and no stranger to trouble, but now we had to think about Ethan.

Otis was carrying a shotgun with him these days, and he was a mighty tough man in a knuckle-and-skull fight. I know, because I had fought him one time. I'm glad I don't have to do that again.

The ranch is a big place, with a lot of ground to cover. That's where Dugan and his mining buddies came in. They all felt they owed me for cleaning up the highwaymen and outlaws who had robbed the miners on these trails around Silverton, and Dugan promised to bring all the help we needed.

In town, Holt had somebody to watch the *Suds 'n Such*, and he would help Sarge patrol and keep the peace in Silverton. I was satisfied on both fronts. That just left me to find and bring in this man who had invaded my property.

My ticket was just to Alamosa, at least on this first leg of the trip. I would get off the train there and see what I could learn. There were three rail lines out of

Alamosa. I couldn't afford not to check on all three, even though the first two seemed unlikely.

The sandy-haired man could have taken the train west to South Fork. Even though I felt sure he had been in on the raid at the Flying W out there, I didn't think he had any reason to go back there now. His gang had been arrested, and he was on the run.

The second rail line went south to Antonito. I couldn't think of why he would go south unless he was getting out of the state. If so, good riddance. He could just keep going to Mexico for all I cared.

The third line went to the east and northeast. He could ride to Pueblo and continue from there to Denver, or he could take another train to Salida. I was betting on that one—the one to Salida. I felt in my pocket and came out with the map I'd had drawn for me by the old man in the saloon in Salida. A hideout in the mountains. That sounded likely to me.

As the train began its climb to the snowy peaks of the San Juan Mountains, I stretched out and closed my eyes. I had learned a long time ago to get some sleep when I could. You never knew what might happen tomorrow.

I stepped down from the train in Salida, collected my horse, and rode straight to the general store. I was still working on hunches because I didn't have much else to go on.

The railroad clerk back at Alamosa had looked like he'd spent his lunch hour down at the local saloon.

He'd been useless to me. I asked about the sandy-haired man, and he stared at me without blinking until I thought he had gone to sleep. Finally, he blinked and nodded.

"Yep, I think I saw a feller like that. Sandy hair, checked shirt, duster coat...yep." He went back to staring at me. "Where did he go? Uh...he bought him a ticket outta here. To, uh..."

His voice trailed away, and his eyes went a little out of focus. He shrugged. "Mighta been Pueblo, or South Fork." He rocked back and forth on his heels and seemed to forget what the question was.

So, I had bought tickets through to Salida and now I was going to the general store. It was late afternoon, the day after I had left Silverton. I was gambling that this outlaw was going to hole up in a hideout up there, and he would need some supplies and such to get by.

The little bell went off when I stepped inside the store, and I could see right away that the owner remembered me from before. He waved and stepped from behind the counter, walked over, and extended a hand.

"Whaddya need?"

I glanced around to make sure the store was empty. "I want to ask whether a fella came through here and bought supplies in the last day." I gave him the same description I had been giving to railroad clerks.

He started nodding his head up and down before I finished, and my hopes rose. "About this time yestiddy, he come in and bought him some supplies. Food and a little ammo and such."

His brow furrowed, and he frowned. "Is he a bad 'un?" he asked me.

"Might be," I agreed. "You got any reason to think he is?"

He heaved a sigh. "Yeah, the last thing he bought weren't the usual stuff. Mind you, he maybe needs to clear a tree stump or open a path or sumthin'." He led me to the back of the store and pointed at a box high on the shelf. It had a sign on it: *Dynamite.*

It was too late in the afternoon to do much more today. I took a quick tour around Salida. I didn't see anybody answering to my quarry's description, and I didn't expect to. Returning to the general store, I got myself some hardtack and jerky. I expected to be on the trail by daybreak.

After a quick dinner at a café, I went to the room I had taken at a boardinghouse and took out the map I'd gotten from the old-timer at the saloon the last time I had come to Salida. I spread it out on the bed and brought the candle closer for a better look.

It was pretty clear I would follow the Arkansas River out of town, moving toward the mountains. As the trail climbed and wound into the mountains, I was sure it would get narrower and more faint. I shook my head and folded up the map. Rains that had come through a few days ago would help me follow a trail, if there was a trail. I was counting on that.

Daylight found me in the saddle and on the trail, following the glint reflecting off the Arkansas River in the early morning sun. There was a lot of traffic to and from mining camps for a while, so I didn't spend a lot of time looking at tracks. There were too many of 'em. It was almost two hours later that the tracks thinned out. I dismounted and checked the few remaining tracks more closely as I went.

The trail rose through high meadows and into the foothills. There were only two sets of tracks in front of me now. They both stayed on the trail, so I wasn't forced to choose which to follow. One horse looked to have a missing nail in the shoe on the right fore-leg. I wasn't sure what that told me. It could be a rider who didn't look after his horse, or it could be somebody who had ridden a long and hard trail lately.

I stopped around noon to eat and to water Buck in a cold spring that crossed the trail. Pushing on, I climbed into the mountains for another hour and finally came to a place on the trail where I had to make a choice. The tracks I'd been following had gone in two different directions.

I stopped to make my decision. I used my binoculars to see what lay in each direction, stepping back under the cover of the trees to do so. One path seemed to lead down into a box canyon. The other looked more like a game trail, leading higher and deeper into the mountains. I could see a very narrow ledge or two along that trail.

The horse with the missing nail in his shoe had gone to the left, on the narrow game trail, climbing higher. I sighed, checked the map, and climbed into the saddle. The narrow trail seemed more likely. I slowed the pace, making sure Buck could pick his footing very carefully.

Coming around a switchback on the trail, I reined Buck in suddenly. There was a narrow ledge in front of me, and there was something about the rock face on the cliff walls in front of me that looked funny. I could see what looked like a shack built against the wall. It could have covered a cave entrance.

I grabbed my binoculars, swung down, and pulled Buck to the side of the trail. I hadn't moved a minute too soon. The whine of a bullet zipped past me. I ducked and disappeared into the brush, putting cedar trees between me and whoever was shooting. A few minutes later, I tethered Buck, pulled my Winchester, and crawled back toward the trail on hands and knees.

Sprawling in the brush, I got my first look through the glasses. Sure enough, there was a shack built against the cliff wall, and I was betting it led to a cave. There was something that looked like a peephole in the door of that shack. I was betting he'd taken a pot shot through that peephole. I hadn't forgotten that the guy I was tracking had bought him some dynamite in Salida, either.

There was no chance at all that I was crossing that narrow ledge in the daylight. I wasn't too keen on sneakin' across there at night, either. Too much moonlight to give him a chance at another shot.

I laid there in the brush for a while and did some thinkin' about this. I had me a nervous guy in that shack over there. He was worried about somebody following him. That made him trigger-happy. That part wasn't good. The good part was that nervous, guilty men do stupid things sometimes. At least I could make him more nervous than he already was.

I scooched over a little to my left and laid my Winchester over a fallen log, sighting down the barrel through the brush. It wouldn't be a problem at all to put a few bullets into that door.

I looked down at the Colt in my belt, then looked off to the right. I could crawl back and forth, taking shots with the Winchester and then the Colt. Maybe he would think there was more than one of me after him.

I fired off two shots from the Winchester into that door, crawled over to the Colt, and fired two more, hearing the shots ricochet off the rock face. Then I crawled back to the Winchester and took a gander through the glasses. Maybe he would do something stupid, like stick his fool head out that door.

EIGHT
FULTON'S FOLLY

W es Fulton had watched every passenger
boarding his trains for two days, then he'd
watched his back trail all the way to the hideout. He'd
seen nothing, but he was jumpier than ever.

There had been only two stops in Salida before
riding to his hideout. The first stop was at the general
store, where he'd bought hardtack, jerky, some ammo,
matches, and exactly two sticks of dynamite.

The second stop had been at a saloon, where he
bought two bottles of whiskey. He was wishing now
he'd bought three or four. The first bottle was halfway
gone when he reached the hideout. Now there were
only a few swallows left in the bottom of that bottle.
He kept the second one within easy reach.

Fulton had just one reason for buying the dynamite. Actually, he'd bought the whiskey for mostly the
same reason. He couldn't shake the image of the posse
stringing up Ace Musgrove and pushing him off the
Larimer Street Bridge in Denver. He could see it in his

mind just as clearly now as he saw it the night it happened.

The darkness in the shack was scary, but there wasn't much he could do about it. There was no way to get any light into the shack unless he opened that door at the entrance. There was no chance he was doing that. Not for a few days, anyway. That's why he had the candles and matches.

His guns, ammo, and the two sticks of dynamite were near the front wall of the shack. Every few minutes, he checked to be sure they were still there when he checked through his peephole in the front door. He'd seen nobody all day, but there were still several hours to go before sundown.

When the first bottle of whiskey was empty, he reached for the second. After a few swigs, Fulton felt overwhelmingly tired and laid down on the floor for a few seconds. When he came awake an hour later, he swore, pushed himself to his feet, and staggered over to look through the peephole.

He looked, jumped back, swore again, then stepped up for another look. There was somebody out there! He could see a guy on horseback. Fulton turned and grabbed his Winchester, aimed, and fired a shot through the peephole. The guy disappeared, but Fulton didn't think he'd hit anything.

He screwed up his courage enough to take another look through the peephole. He couldn't see anything, but he staggered back and fell when he heard rifle shots and two bullets thudded against the door. Moments later, shots sounded again, and he could hear bullets whining and ricocheting off the canyon walls.

How many of them were there? Fulton slumped to the floor next to his guns and the dynamite, clutching the candle and the fresh bottle of whiskey. It was quiet out there now, but that didn't make him feel any better.

He took several swigs of the whiskey and felt a little calmer. Two more swigs and the room started to swim around. Fulton slumped to the floor, reached out to touch the dynamite, and relaxed. They would never take him alive the way they had taken Ace Musgrove. He would take them with him.

Fulton was trying to lever himself back to his feet to look out the front door again when he blacked out. He slumped to the floor of the shack. He never felt it when the candle slipped from his grasp. The wick on one stick of dynamite sputtered and burned.

Fulton came awake just long enough to see the wick burning down to the dynamite. He reached out to grab it, but he couldn't focus well enough to put out the flame.

⊏⊐

After I had loosed the four rounds at the door, I settled back to wait. No telling what this guy would do, so I wasn't sticking my head up above the brush. I watched the peephole through the sights of my Winchester. If I saw a barrel come through that peephole, I would make things downright uncomfortable for him.

I thought I heard a low rumble just before the explosion. There was a flash of light, then an enormous blast. I ducked and grabbed my hat. Small pebbles landed on my head. Chunks of wood filled the air, some of them on fire. Dust and more pebbles came next, then an enormous cloud of smoke billowed out from the shack.

I covered my head with my hands and buried my face in the brush. I could hear rocks landing on the ledge in front of me. Luckily, they didn't seem to reach me. I didn't need rocks raining down on me. Pebbles were bad enough. After a while, I raised my head and risked a look at the shack.

Buck was snorting and pawing the ground. I couldn't blame him. I trotted over to calm him down, then went back to get a look at the shack.

It wasn't there anymore. What was left of it was on fire. The wind was carrying away most of the dust. I could see well enough to make out the entrance to a cave at the back of the shack, so I was right about that. It was a shack that had extended back into a natural cave.

I stayed down for another ten minutes, then stood and walked to the edge of the narrow ledge I had stayed away from earlier. It was no use looking to see who had been in there when the dynamite went off. There couldn't be anything left of him, and I didn't have the stomach for a close-up look inside.

My hat was covered with dust. I stood there for a while, trying to slap the dust off me. I slapped my hat against my leg a few times and put it back on my head, still staring at where that shack used to be.

A moment later, I turned and walked back to mount up. There was just enough time to get back to Salida before dark. I couldn't be sure who had died in there, but I knew that a guy answering to the description I'd been given had bought dynamite in Salida and had somehow blown himself up with it.

I couldn't see how there was anything else I needed to know. The head rustler, whoever he was, had died in an explosion, so far as I was concerned. It was time to get home to the ranch.

━━━

Matt Warner met up with the Castle brothers, Bryce and Tom, at the same place where they always met when they were in Denver. The back room at the *Dead Man's Whiskey* saloon was always open to them. That was because the owner could tell anybody getting rough in the saloon that the Castle gang liked to spend time at this place. That was usually enough to make a man think twice before he pulled his pistol. Once in a while, Warner had to deal with somebody, and word got around when he did. The lesson: you drank your whiskey and didn't cause trouble in *Dead Man's Whiskey*.

Warner strolled down Larimer Street, moving toward *Dead Man's Whiskey*. This area was full of gambling houses, saloons, and several other places where a man could get in trouble. Warner wasn't worried about those. He stayed away from them. You just had to watch out for somebody drunk enough and stupid enough to pull his smokewagon when you weren't looking.

Nobody gave him any trouble today. He walked past several drunks on the street, but they were mostly passed out. He stopped once to look behind him. It was never a bad idea to check your backtrail, even in town. There was nobody following him.

Warner reached the saloon and pushed through the doors. The barkeep nodded and tilted his head at the back room. Warner took that to mean the Castle brothers were here and waiting for him. Warner tapped on the door and went in.

There was a third man who was there already, along with the Castle brothers. Warner stopped and stared, then looked over at Bryce Castle, who shrugged. "My sister's kid, Harvey," he explained. "Harvey's gonna ride with us for a while."

Matt took a seat and didn't bother any further with the kid. He could be the Castle brothers' problem. If the kid gave Warner any trouble, there were ways to set up a man to take a bullet during a robbery.

This was an important meeting. The three of them hadn't planned or pulled a robbery since the one at the bank in Telluride last year. That one had gone so well that they had gone different directions and spent their money for a while. Now they needed more.

The three of them had gone to three different towns to get the lay of the land before coming to this meeting. It had to be a bank robbery—they had decided on that a long time ago. Planning was what they did, and bank robberies were the easiest to plan. The bank wasn't going anywhere like a train or a stagecoach.

They knew everything about the bank and the town before they made a move.

Now they had all scouted their banks and towns. Warner had gone to Silverton, Tom Castle to Leadville, and Bryce Castle to Durango. It was time to decide which bank to rob. Warner waited for one of the brothers to go first.

"Leadville looks good." Tom Castle swung his boots down from the table to the floor. "Lotsa mining money in that town. First National Bank of Leadville looks ripe for the takin'." He stopped to light a cigar. "One sheriff, no deputy, no militia around there since they taken down a gang robbin' miners on the trails around town. Quiet now."

Bryce Castle rubbed his chin, listening. "Best way outta town?"

His brother thought for a while. "East and south along the Arkansas River. We could come down through Salida or over to Fairplay. Could catch a train somewhere after that."

"What happened with the militia and the road gang?" his brother asked. Warner could tell that Bryce Castle looked doubtful.

Tom shrugged. "Big road gang paid off the mayor and maybe the sheriff. A marshal come in with a deputy marshal and some militia. Taken down the whole gang. Mayor's gone, new sheriff. Town has quieted down. They even ran Soapy Smith out of town."

Bryce Castle nodded and turned to Warner. "Silverton?"

"Real good. Only one bank, Bank of Silverton, but

lots of mining around there, lots of folks comin' and goin' from the bank. One sheriff, he might be kinda salty, but there's just him. There's some good money in that town."

"How do we get out?" This came from Tom Castle.

"West. Out along the Animas River valley, maybe fifty miles to Durango. We can take a train there to anywhere we want."

"Why not catch a train there in Silverton? We could get out fast." Harvey's mouth was open to say more, but the three looks he got from the others made him change his mind.

"One guy watchin' the station, that's all they would need," Bryce snarled. "He could cut down all four of us if he's ready and we ain't lookin' for him." He turned to look at the others. "Durango ain't a mining town," he said, but there's still money around from the trains coming through and all the businesses. I maybe like it the best. They don't watch the bank there like they watch 'em in them mining towns. Maybe we can catch 'em by surprise at the bank and get out. We ride south into New Mexico and work our way to El Paso. We go where we want from there."

Bryce Castle reached out for the whiskey bottle on the table, poured himself a drink, and passed it around. The others just waited. Bryce was the planner. He stroked his mustache, staring at the wall and thinking out loud.

"Mebbe we could hit Silverton, ride over to Durango, lie low for a while, then hit Durango and get outta the state. For good."

"What about the law?" Warner objected. "Marshals, sheriffs, deputies, militia. Won't they be lookin' out for us in Durango so soon after we take down the bank in Silverton? They can send the militia on trains and git there in a hurry if they smell trouble." Warner wasn't sure he'd been heard at first. Bryce Castle was still staring at the wall and stroking his mustache.

Finally, Bryce reached for the bottle again and shifted his gaze to Warner. "Mebbe we make 'em think we're gonna hit Leadville and throw 'em off the scent. They can rush the marshals and the sojer boys up to Leadville while we take down Durango." He looked over at Harvey. "That could be where you come in, kid."

The telegram caught up with me at the train station in Salida. Wouldn't you just know it? I had finished up with the rustlers, and I was on my way home for a week of rounding up cattle and branding. I might even have a few steers to sell this year, and I had me an idea on how to get 'em over to Durango for sale.

I sighed and opened the telegram. It was from Brad Anderson, but it was really from Governor Pritkin. He just got Brad to send the telegram, that's all. Now I knew how this worked. The governor wanted to meet with me, Brad Anderson, and a couple other guys at the governor's office the day after tomorrow.

I sighed again and bought a ticket to get me to Denver instead of going home to Silverton. I mentally kicked myself a couple times for the telegram I'd sent to Brad Anderson yesterday, telling him the last rustler had paid his dues. The governor likely had something else he wanted me to do now. I planned to say no.

Brad met me at the train station in Denver the next afternoon. I looked pretty shabby for the meeting with the governor in the morning, but I wasn't going to worry about that. He'd called me in from off the trail.

Brad took me to a steakhouse for dinner and told me the state of Colorado was paying for it. That sounded good to me, but I wondered again what it was they wanted me to do. Brad wouldn't say. I tried it another way.

"Who's gonna be at that meeting tomorrow besides you and me and the governor, Brad?"

He squirmed a little, then told me there would be two guys from the Denver & Rio Grande Railroad. One of them would be the president of the line. The other guy was apparently in charge of their security.

I digested that news for a minute, along with my steak. "They're worried about getting robbed, huh?"

Brad just nodded. After a minute, he had a suggestion. "I know you don't want my job, Lat, but if you have ideas that'll help those railroad boys and the governor feel secure about all that money moving around on the trains, that'll help. You were always the man with the ideas."

Well, I don't know if my ideas were that good, but I sat back and waited for my apple pie and thought. I sat up when something rang a little bell in my head. Brad was watching me.

"What?"

"Have you got a Pinkerton's office in Denver?" I asked.

Brad nodded and told me where to find it. I decided to visit them first thing in the morning.

———

When I arrived at the governor's office the next morning at ten o'clock, I had the manager of the Colorado office of Pinkerton's with me. He hadn't been invited to the meeting, so I asked him to sit out in the lobby for a minute. I had a feeling they would be glad to talk to him later.

Governor Pritkin welcomed me to his office and introduced me to a guy named Abe Froman, president of the Denver & Rio Grande Railroad. The guy in charge of security shook my hand after Abe Froman got done.

The governor waved me into a chair and got right down to it.

"Lat, you wrapped up that rustler thing slicker'n anything I've seen lately. I've got to ask one more time, will you come and help us keep Colorado safe, working as a marshal?"

I shook my head. He seemed to expect it. "I'm sorry, Governor Pritkin, but I'm just a rancher these days. What I did on that rustler case was just because my town and home were threatened."

The governor nodded and glanced over at Brad Anderson. "Brad told me that's what you would say, but I to try." He folded his hands on his desktop.

"Okay, if you have any tips or ideas to help us stay ahead of the outlaws, can you give 'em to us now?"

"Pinks on the trains." I was watching Abe Froman while I said it, and his head was already shaking side to side. Those boys don't like to spend money.

"What if a Pinkerton agent could stop just one big robbery of a shipment of ore or money?" I asked. "Wouldn't that be worth it? There are railroads all over the west using Pinkerton's."

Governor Pritkin turned his gaze on Abe Froman. "What about it, Abe? You can't expect the state to cover all your trains with militiamen. We'll help, but you have to help yourself."

I could see him caving in a little, so I went to the door and invited my guest into the meeting. "Carlton Boone, from the Pinkertons' office here in Denver. Let him tell you what he can do for you."

Half an hour later, Froman had agreed to use Pinkerton's services. I had one more idea before we wrapped it up. I turned to Carlton Boone. "Who draws those wanted posters we have in the sheriff's offices?"

Boone shrugged. "Well, there are various artists who do that. Sometimes they work for the county or a city. We have one we use here in Denver from time to time."

I leaned forward. "I know the wanted posters are for somebody that already killed somebody or robbed a train or something, but what if we had drawings of people we think might be planning to kill or rob? Or somebody that probably did, but we can't be sure of it yet? We could send a poster around to be on the lookout for that face. Pinkertons could share the posters with the marshals and sheriffs. Maybe we could stop something before it happens."

Fifteen minutes later, it was all set up. Descriptions could be sent to Pinkerton's artist, and marshals and militia would share the drawings.

My work was done now. I even turned down lunch with Brad and the governor to catch the next train home. I figured these guys could get along just fine without me.

This is why I'm not a fortune teller. I can't even see what's coming when there's trouble headed right for me.

NINE
SILVERTON STRIKE

You couldn't really call branding an annual event around my ranch, since this was only the third year we'd had any calves to brand. The first year, there were only two. Last year, there were six. This year, I was thinking we had thirteen calves to brand.

Otis and I had spent two days driving the herd down to the lower pasture. I had ridden among 'em, and that's how I came up with the number thirteen. It seemed like we might need to start building some kind of a branding corral for next year, but I figured our regular horse corral could handle it this year.

Joanna cooked up a feast for this day, and I got Holt to hand over the *Suds 'n Such* to his bartender so he could come to help. Sarge decided the town was safe enough for him to come and join in, so we had four hands for the branding.

We lined up at the top of the pasture and drove them down slowly, cutting out the unbranded calves and driving them into the corral. Joanna handled the gate while Ethan took a nap in the cradle we had brought out from the house.

The corral wasn't big enough for all thirteen, so we drove in only half at a time. Where one or two of them proved too slippery to be driven in, I had to shake out a loop and rope 'em.

Otis was the one who wrestled them to the ground while I did the branding, since Otis was almost as big as the calves himself. With a herd as small as mine still is, we had finished by a little past noon, when we were rewarded with Joanna's lunch.

It was my plan on how to sell the five steers that had everybody interested around the ranches in Silverton. All the ranches around here could benefit from this if my plan worked.

With that in mind, the four of us cut out the five steers after lunch and started them down the trail to town. With four of us and only five of them, it wasn't that hard to keep them in line.

We drove them to the railroad depot in Silverton and then into a stock corral. As far as I knew, the Denver & Rio Grande Railroad hadn't yet taken any cattle on the narrow-gauge rails. For sure, there hadn't been any steers taken to Durango by rail from Silverton. I had convinced the stationmasters here in Silverton and in Durango to give it a try.

We waited for the train to come in. Sarge went back to his office, but Holt, Otis, and I watched and waited. Otis would ride the train to Durango, sell the cows, and take the train home tomorrow.

At last, the train rolled in, and we watched while a dozen or so passengers stepped down. The last man off the train seemed familiar. He was tall, dark-haired, and walked with his head down and his hat pulled low. He glanced my way as he stepped into the depot and the hair went up on the back of my neck. It was that scar down the side of his face that I remembered.

I had seen him here in Silverton a little while back, and he'd gotten my attention last time, too. I watched as he walked over to claim his horse, then mounted and rode out of town without looking back.

I reminded myself I had only seen him twice and he'd done nothing wrong that I knew of. I went over and watched the railroad people load my cattle, then told Otis to go and enjoy himself as he boarded the train.

Holt and I were leaving the depot when I heard my name. I turned and saw the stationmaster trotting toward me with a piece of paper in his hand. He gave me the paper.

"Your buyer is ready to take the cows in Durango," he said. He turned to go.

"Do all your train stations have a telegraph?" I asked.

He nodded. "Pretty near all of 'em got a telegraph machine and telegraph operator," he told me.

"Okay," I said. I had seen the telegraph lines running next to the rails on most of the train routes, so it sounded like the railroads were ahead of the towns in getting telegraph services put in. It was something to remember. Maybe it could come in handy someday.

Part of my brain was still churning, thinking about that guy with the scar on his face. I had seen him leave town, but if he came back, I might look into what he was doing around here.

Walking over to the *Suds 'n Such* with Holt for a beer, I remembered my idea about having the Pinkerton artist draw and circulate pictures of people we thought might be up to no good. I wondered if I should have a picture drawn of the guy I had just seen, then shook off the thought. Maybe the scar just made him look like more trouble than he really was.

Matt Warner collected his horse and rode straight out of town. That hadn't been his plan to start with. He had planned on getting a room in town and waiting for the Castle brothers and their nephew to roll in tomorrow and start planning the robbery.

That was before that same guy had been there at the station, watching him. The tall guy with the eyes that didn't miss anything. Warner had seen that guy before, watching him. Something told him this guy was trouble. Besides, Warner liked to slip in and out of towns with nobody noticing or remembering him. Without thinking, he touched the scar on the side of his face. The scar was the only thing that made it difficult.

The tents and temporary shacks of the miners passing through town were on the south side of Silverton. He remembered that from his last visit. He would toss down a bedroll out there and stay out of sight for the night.

Warner reached the miner's shantytown and found

a spot for his bedroll. He tossed it down and straightened up to look around. The train tracks were nearby, running south toward Durango. On an impulse, he mounted up to follow the tracks.

A few miles outside of town, the tracks rose sharply and curved around a bend. Warner reined in his horse and studied the tracks. The train would have to slow down to get up that rise and around the bend.

Looking to his left, he saw the entrance to what looked like an old silver mine. Warner rode up to the mine entrance, dismounted, and looked around. The cave they had dug out for mining ran only about two hundred yards into the mountainside, then stopped abruptly. It looked like they had decided this one wouldn't pay out and moved on.

Warner looked around one more time, then mounted and rode back to the shantytown. He was tired enough that even dozens of rowdy miners with a snootful of whiskey wouldn't keep him awake tonight.

The Castle brothers and the kid nephew named Harvey were on the eleven o'clock train the next morning, just as Warner expected. He lounged against the wall of the depot while they collected their horses, then he led the way to the café, staying several yards in front of them.

Leading the way to the back of the café, Harvey took a seat facing the door. The scarred side of his face was next to the side wall. A quick glance around the room told him nobody seemed to be watching them.

He relaxed and listened as Bryce Castle handed out the duties he expected them to get done in the next few days.

Tom Castle and Warner were to work out the escape route out of town. Warner's eyebrows rose a little when Bryce said they wouldn't have a set of fresh horses ready, just in case they had a posse hot on their tail. They were to figure out how to cover their tracks thoroughly with no need for a change of horses. Somewhere between here and Durango, they would disappear for a couple of weeks.

Bryce asked for questions. Both Warner and Tom Castle shook their heads. They had no questions. Warner kept his head down as he dug into a plate of eggs, waiting to hear what Bryce and Harvey, the kid nephew, would do this week.

When Bryce told the kid he would go into the bank to open an account and scout out the setup inside, Warner's eyebrows rose again. After the robbery, the face that the bank clerks might remember when asked about any unknown faces would be Harvey's. Bryce didn't seem to mind putting his nephew in danger.

Bryce himself would scout the town, watching the bank and deciding on the best time to strike. Midday was usually the best, but Bryce would keep his ear to the ground in the saloons and general store to see if he could find out about the railroad payroll or anything else that might fatten up the contents of the vault.

Harvey, after opening an account and getting a look inside the bank, was to set up the distraction. They always used a distraction—usually an explosion or a fire. That got any potential heroes and maybe the sheriff running in the other direction. Bryce gave the kid a little money to buy an old wagon and some hay. He would start a fire in the hay wagon at the edge of town.

They wouldn't be meeting again in town. They would meet up in two days at sundown outside of town. Warner suggested they follow the train tracks south out of town until they saw an abandoned mine near the tracks. They would meet there.

The meeting at the mine ironed out the last details of the robbery. Two days later, Warner was sitting on the edge of town between Tom and Bryce Castle, waiting for the school bell to chime, signaling it was time to move in.

Warner's one last effort to convince Bryce Castle to plan for a fresh set of horses as a robbery getaway hadn't gone well. Warner's face settled into a frown as he remembered Bryce yelling at him when he'd suggested it. Warner glanced at Bryce sideways, but Castle was staring down at the town, just waiting for the signal from the school bell.

Warner and Tom Castle had laid out the escape route, and Warner had to admit things looked pretty good. They would ride for a mile or two outside of Silverton, then wade their horses along the Animas River for about a mile.

There, a rocky ledge on the western side of the river gave them the perfect place to climb out of the river without leaving tracks. They would quickly reach the cover of spruce trees, and the terrain then rose sharply into the San Juan Mountains. They could take cover on the first mesa that presented itself and have a commanding field of fire against any posse foolish enough to follow them that far.

Bryce had scouted the town and the bank. There was a steady stream of money coming in from the miners. Bryce had decided that a Monday would be the best day. The Bank of Silverton would be fat with the money spent by the miners over the weekend.

Harvey had bought an old hay wagon and hidden it near the train into town on the north side. He needed only a few minutes to haul it to the edge of town and set the hay on fire as a diversion.

That left just the matter of coordinating the hay fire with the attack on the bank. Like a lot of western towns, the school met in the church during the week. Plans to build a school were going slowly.

School in Silverton started and ended early. The kids were needed for chores at home, so school started at seven a.m. and ended at three in the afternoon. Lunch was at eleven. The school bell rang at those three times.

Bryce had decided the perfect time to hit the bank would be at eleven, and the school bell would be their signal. Harvey would set the hay on fire and the other three would move in on the bank at precisely that time.

On edge, waiting for the signal, Warner's eyes swept Main Street, and he saw something that put a smile on his face. He pointed, then saw both Castles nodding and grinning. The sheriff was riding out of town.

When the first chime of the school sounded five minutes later, Warner and the Castles were moving.

━━━

Otis had returned on the early train this morning with great news about the sale of my steers. Beef prices can come and go, but there was a great demand right now, and Otis had sold my five steers for top dollar—forty dollars apiece!

I was shoeing a horse in the corral when Otis came back with that news, and I let out a whoop. It was almost twice what I had thought I would get. I knew just what I wanted to do with the money.

Joanna had run a bakery in town for a few years when we first came here, and it had done well. When little Ethan came along, though, she had sold the bakery to a lady in town. We had spent the money fixing up a room for Ethan and on livestock for the ranch.

I knew Joanna missed spending time in town like she had done when she owned the bakery. This money would go toward a trip to Denver. When Ethan was a little older and could travel better, we would take the train to Denver, stay in a nice hotel, and eat in the best places.

I gave Otis twenty dollars for making the trip and for doing so well with the sale. He grinned and stuffed the money in his pocket. "Any time, boss," he rumbled.

I looked at the money left in my hand and thought that it would be just about right for the trip I had in mind. Prices were higher in the city, but I wouldn't be cheap about this. Joanna deserved the best.

I had just about spent that money in my head when I heard a lot of hollerin' and commotion. I looked out toward the trail and saw a lot of dust coming my way. As the rider got closer, I saw it was Barney, the big, awkward redheaded kid Holt used to help him out at the *Suds 'n Such.*

I watched as Barney rode up to the corral and just about launched himself out of the saddle. He ran toward me, then stumbled and grabbed the rails of the corral to steady himself. When Barney was real nervous, he stuttered.

"Bbbbb-bank robbers!" he shouted. "In town!" He pointed toward Silverton to show me where, but I knew that part already. "Bbbb-bank robbers! Holt sent me to git you! There's been a buncha shots fired!".

I had already swung around and grabbed my saddle from the corral rail. I turned to yell at Otis. "Watch the ranch," I hollered. I finished saddling Buck and swung aboard. "Tell Joanna!" I grabbed my Winchester and stuffed it into the scabbard. It went without saying that I wore my Colt everywhere.

I put my heels to Buck's flanks, and we galloped toward Silverton.

━━━

So far, the robbery was running like clockwork. That made Warner a little nervous at first, but then he remembered the job they had done at Telluride a year ago. Lots of cash, the posse had dropped off in no time, and they had made a clean getaway with plenty of money in their pockets. Maybe today would be like that.

There had been only four customers in the bank and no traffic in the streets when they'd come in. Most of the people on Main Street had gone down to help put out the fire in the hay wagon.

Now, with all four customers lying on the ground with their hands over their heads, Warner had the tellers empty their drawers into a burlap sack he carried to each station.

Tom Castle held his pistol on the customers while Bryce marched the bank manager to the vault and held a gun on him while he turned the dial. When the vault was open, the manager laid down on the floor next to the customers.

Warner finished emptying the cash drawers, then he ordered the tellers to lie face down on the floor. There were two women and one man, they dropped to their knees to do what they'd been told. Warner waited impatiently for Bryce to finish in the vault. He turned to look out the front window. Harvey had arrived and was holding their horses as ordered.

Warner heard somebody coming out of the vault. He turned to see Bryce trotting toward him, twisting shut the top of the burlap sack he'd used to hold the loot. An alarm rang in Warner's brain—something was wrong.

He looked toward the tellers. The male teller had pulled a gun from his boot and was lifting the pistol!

Warner fired immediately, smashing the teller back against the desk behind him. The gun still dangled from the teller's fingers, and Warner fired again. The gun fell to the floor and the teller slid down the side of the desk.

"Out!" Bryce thundered, and they dashed through the front door. When they reached the porch, Warner grabbed the reins of his horse and leaped on. As he turned his horse, there was a gunshot from across the street. Warner felt a searing pain across his shoulder.

There was a guy at the entrance of the saloon down the street, holding a Winchester! Warner fired and saw the man spinning away and falling back through the saloon entrance.

All four thundered out of town and on the trail toward Durango. Warner cursed loudly as he played it back in his head. He had killed one man and put a bullet into another. This one hadn't been as clean as Telluride. He ignored the pain in his shoulder as they galloped past the miner's shantytown. They couldn't get to the river soon enough.

TEN
HITTING HOME

I pushed Buck to his limit to get to town, leaving
Barney somewhere behind me by the time I
galloped up to the bank. Still, it was all over, just as I
had feared. I swung down and dashed up to the door
just in time to see them wheeling somebody out.

Sarge followed the cart out and came over to stand
beside me as they wheeled the cart toward the barbershop. I knew what that meant. The alley behind the
barbershop was where they kept the coffins.

"Bert Lipscomb," Sarge said in a low tone.

I turned in surprise. Bert was a young guy, maybe
only twenty or twenty-one and he hadn't been
working there for more than six months. "How?" was
the only question I could think of.

"They said he pulled a pistol out of his boot," Sarge
said grimly.

I shook my head and watched as they wheeled the
cart away.

"There's more bad news," Sarge said. He pointed

toward Doc Adams's office, down the street. "Holt got off a shot with his rifle outside the *Suds 'n Such*. They returned fire and put a bullet in his arm. Doc's working on him now."

I was torn, staring down the street at the trail they'd likely taken out of here, then looking over at the doc's office.

"Go ahead and check on him," Sarge murmured. "They've been gone at least twenty minutes. I just got back in town myself. They have had time to get out on the trail, cover their tracks in the river and mebbe git themselves forted up out there in the hills. I don't plan on a posse. Mebbe you an' me can track 'em for a ways after you check on Holt."

I nodded and trotted across the street and down to the doc's office. I knocked on my way through the door. Doc was just coming from the back room, wiping the blood from his hands. He dropped into a chair and told me to do the same.

"I got the bullet out," he said grimly. "He'll have some healin' up to do, but I think he'll come out of it okay." He gestured toward the back room. "He passed out when I got the bullet. Maybe he'll sleep for a while now. Best thing for him."

I twisted my hat in my hands, wondering what else I should do for Holt. Doc pointed at the door. "I'll take care of him," he said. "Sarge probably needs you now. Don't you boys get yourselves shot. I don't need no more patients."

I dashed out the door and went back to the bank. Sarge was mounted up and holding Buck's reins when I got there. I didn't say anything, just took the lead out of town, following the tracks. Of the two of us, I was the better tracker.

For the first fifteen minutes, we moved at a fast trot. There were four sets of recent tracks, which matched what they had told Sarge at the bank. Four robbers, three inside and one holding the reins to the horses outside.

After fifteen minutes, the tracks disappeared. They didn't just fade away, they disappeared, and it wasn't hard to figure out what had happened. The tracks led to the edge of the river. They had walked their horses down the Animas River to cover their tracks.

"Same thing I would have done," I muttered. Sarge nodded. He had already guessed this part.

We walked our horses down the riverbank, watching for any place they might have left the river. After fifteen minutes, we reined in while I looked up uneasily at the mountain peaks on both sides. Sharp inclines led up from the river, with stands of cedar trees, followed by mesas and craggy cliff faces.

"We could be smack dab in the middle of a shootin' gallery pretty soon," Sarge commented. He leaned over to spit. "Besides that," he told me, "I'm out of my jurisdiction right about here. San Juan County ends and La Plata County begins. I can't do nothing more." He looked at me sideways. "A marshal, now, he could do something more."

I soaked that up and said nothing for a while. Sarge was right about both things, but I was boiling inside. Somebody should have to pay for Bert and Holt. Finally, I nodded and reined Buck around.

"Have you told Brad Anderson, or somebody with the governor's office?" I asked.

Sarge shook his head. "I thought maybe you should be the one to do that," he answered.

We rode and said nothing most of the way back. When we reached the edge of Silverton, I asked if Sarge had talked to anybody at the bank about the robbers, getting descriptions and things like that.

Sarge shook his head. "I'd just got there when you came. We can go over and talk to folks now. I told Mort to keep everybody there until we get back."

Mort Owens, the bank president, had kept everybody there. I went to the tellers first, then talked to Mort. Nobody was much help. They wore bandanas and hats. One teller said the guy taking their money from the cages had light-blue eyes. Well, that was something.

I asked Mort about new faces around the bank lately and his head came up. "Yeah, young fella," he said. "Just a few days ago. Maybe only twenty, twenty-one. I don't see many folks that young open a new account."

I pressed him for a description.

Mort stared at the ceiling and thought. "Light-colored hair, like dark blonde or light brown. Kinda big nose, tall and skinny. Wide shoulders though, like he ain't filled out yet. Big nose, like a checkmark on his face."

I leaned forward. "Was he inside during the robbery?"

Mort shook his head.

I sat back disappointed, then had another thought.

"Could he have been the one holding the horses outside?"

Mort shrugged. "Could be. Nobody got much of a look at him. Maybe about the right height, though."

We were walking out, and I was thinking about having that artist draw a poster when one teller came forward and stopped me.

"This could be nothing," she said slowly.

"Anything you remember could help," I told her.

She nodded. "That guy who took the money from the cages," she said. "His mask slipped a little when he stepped away, and it looked like there was a scar, up high on his cheek. It might have been something you'd really notice if he didn't have a mask."

Now I had something to work with. I left the bank with Sarge, wondering if we had enough of a description on these two to create a poster I could send around to the marshals and Pinkertons. That's when I realized we needed to send a telegram to Brad Anderson. He had about a week left on the job, if I figured it right.

I stepped over to the telegraph office while Sarge went to check on the café and a couple of saloons. He said he would ask if anybody had seen a man with blue eyes and a big scar on his cheek.

I stepped to the counter and began writing out a telegram to Brad. I told him four robbers had hit the Silverton Bank, killing one man and injuring Holt. I told him they had escaped to the south and were out of Sarge's jurisdiction.

I tapped the pencil against the countertop while I thought about what else to say. Finally, I told him I had a little bit of a description of two of them. Could Pinkertons send their sketch artist down here to make posters?

I thought things over, then told the kid behind the desk to send this to Brad Anderson and Governor Pritkin.

When I stepped out of the telegraph office, I saw Sarge moving this way at a fast trot. Come to think of it, Sarge was no spring chicken. That might be a run for Sarge. I'd never seen him run.

Anyway, Sarge came steaming to a stop and pointed at the town café. "Guy with the scar," he blurted, "waitress over there says she saw him. She'll describe him to you. He was there about a week ago."

I dashed over to the café. Sarge trotted along behind me and pointed her out to me when we went into the café. She took her time and thought about it when she described him, which I took as a good sign.

"He never took his hat off, but I'm pretty sure he had dark hair because of the eyebrows," she said. "Those light-blue eyes with dark eyebrows, I remember that. And the scar, it started about here." She pointed to a spot just below her temple. "And it was deep. It ran down into his beard, so I don't know how long it was exactly."

I stepped out of the café with Sarge and told him it was time for me to get back to the ranch. I told him I would be back tomorrow to see if Brad had answered my telegram. Just then, the kid from the telegraph office came out the door and trotted toward me, waving a piece of paper. Brad had answered me already!

Except, when I opened the telegram, it wasn't Brad. It was the governor. I scanned the message.

Latigo Smith,
   Got your telegram. Stop
   I will send the sketch artist if you need him. Stop
   I need to ask one more time. Stop
   Will you come to Denver to talk? Stop
   You can give the description here. Stop
   Will you fill the marshal's job just until
   You can find these men. Stop
   I will send Brad to meet your train. Stop
   Pritkin

Sarge read the telegram over my shoulder. He stepped down to the street, put his hat on, and glanced over at me.

"Looks like you've got some thinkin' to do," he said. He walked away.

I nodded and walked over to unhitch Buck. I needed to go home and talk to Joanna before I answered the governor, but I had a feeling I knew what she would say. She was a western girl, and she knew all about defending your home against lawless men. I had a feeling that's what she would want me to do now.

I walked over, unhitched Buck, mounted up, and headed for home.

━━━

I had ridden these trains several times since I had helped build the rails in Colorado, but never this much. We were in Denver now, and I could see the station up ahead.

My talk with Joanna had gone just the way I had thought it would. She told me to go out there and get the men who attacked our friends in Silverton. I felt my jaw clench down just a tad. I wouldn't stop until I had done just that.

The brakes squealed, the engine gave a loud blast, and I felt the train slow down. By the time we had come to a stop, I had seen Brad Anderson waiting for me out there. I stood up, grabbed my bag, and stepped down to meet Brad.

He shook my hand and led me toward a horse and buggy he had parked across the street. He took a time-piece out of his vest pocket and checked it. "We've got an hour till we talk to the governor," he told me. "Can I getcha something to eat?"

I shook my head. "Not hungry just yet," I said. "Do we have time for me to see the artist you use to make sketches? Think I'd have time to go over a couple of posters with him?"

"It's a her, not a him," Brad said with a grin. "And yeah, I think we've got time." I tossed my bag in the back of the buggy, and he took me to see the artist.

———

It was harder than I thought to describe what somebody looks like well enough for somebody else to draw it. Even the guy with the blue eyes, dark hair, and scar was tough. I had only got a quick look at him twice. The rest of it was just telling her what somebody else had told me. Finally, we got something I thought might be close enough to help.

The tall, skinny youngster with the light-colored hair and a nose like a checkmark on his face was even harder. I just told her to draw him with a thin face and a pointy nose. She drew something that resembled that, and I said it would do. Brad agreed to get copies sent around to Pinkerton and any law enforcement that might need it. Now, we were ready for the governor.

The secretary sent us right in and he was waiting for us. He parked me in a chair across from his desk and got right to it, telling me the state of Colorado needed me, and something had to be done about these outlaws. I started nodding before he was halfway done. He stopped and waited for me to say something.

"I'll do it," I said, "only if you agree to two things."

Governor Pritkin nodded and waited.

"First," I said, "I want the Denver and Rio Grande

Railroad to agree to let me use their telegraph setup and services. I think there will be times when I can get the message out faster with them than I can finding the nearest town with a telegraph office."

Pritkin picked up a pen and made a note. "Done," he said. "I'll get Abe Froman in here and talk to him. Next."

"Two," I said, "I'll just do this until I have brought in the guys who did this in Silverton. You need to keep looking for somebody to take Brad's place as a marshal for after I have gone back to my ranch."

Pritkin squirmed in his seat a little and looked over at Brad. Brad was just staring at the floor. I said nothing else, but I think Pritkin knew I meant it. Finally, he reached his hand across the desk. "Done," he said. We shook hands.

I looked back as Brad and I left the room. The governor had already picked up the piece of paper at the top of his stack and gone to work. I guess it was time for me to get to work too.

━━━

They had taken an old wagon trail south out of Durango. It followed the path of the narrow-gauge railroad line between the two cities. Actually, the railroad had followed the path of the wagon trail.

Warner and Tom Castle had chosen this route for their escape after the holdup. They weren't going to get lost on this trail, but it was far enough from the railroad to avoid being seen. They mostly traveled at night anyway.

The mesa top where they had holed up was about five hundred yards off the wagon trail and another hundred yards about it. It was big enough for the four of them, but Warner couldn't wait to get out of here and move on. According to Bryce Castle, though, that wouldn't be happening soon. Bryce wanted to wait for the kid Harvey to get out there and do a couple things to throw the law off their scent.

It was mostly Harvey that was getting on Warner's nerves. He was a cocky, loudmouthed kid. If they couldn't get off this mesa for a while, at least things would get better when Bryce sent his nephew away.

They were gathered around a campfire now, and Bryce was giving the kid his marching orders.

"You need to get another two or three guys on your crew. You know that many guys you can trust for this?" Bryce stared across the campfire, waiting for his nephew to answer.

"Yeah, I told you already." Harvey looked around, wondering how many times his uncle had asked this question already. "I know some guys back home, they'll help, and I can trust 'em."

Warner fought down his urge to backhand the kid across the face. Instead, he watched Bryce Castle, interested in hearing the plan. Bryce hadn't shared it with Warner. That was another thing Warner was getting tired of.

"Okay, you git your boys together and scare 'em at the bank in Pueblo. Make them think you're gonna rob it. Have a couple of your boys hang around the bank for a day or two. Make 'em nervous. Set off a hay wagon fire like we did in Silverton. Then git outta town. Take the train to Leadville."

Bryce leaned forward to feed a couple more sticks into the fire. Harvey was looking for a stick to whittle, knife in his hand. Bryce glared at him until his nephew looked like he was paying attention.

"When you git to Leadville, you hit the bank there, while everybody is still sniffin' around down in Durango. Do it the same way we done it here. Mebbe use something else to distract 'em. Take your money and git. Stay away from here. You got it?"

Harvey nodded impatiently and scrambled to his feet. Finally, he could get off this godforsaken mesa. Bryce barked one last order as Harvey trotted over to saddle his horse.

"Ten days. You got ten days to do both. We move on Durango in ten days, after you pull all the badges up to Leadville."

Harvey finished saddling his horse and led the gelding down the path off the mesa. He would do most of it like his uncle had said. There were a few things that didn't make much sense to him. He might just change those things.

ELEVEN

THE PUEBLO PROBLEM

H arvey Brown knew exactly where to go to find the guys who would help him pull off the *fake bank robbery* in Pueblo, as well as the real bank robbery in Leadville. He had already decided that both would be real bank robberies. Why go to all that trouble and put yourself in danger if you don't walk away with money both times? He knew his buddies would agree with him.

At the young age of twenty, Harvey was a veteran of all kinds of holdups and outlaw activities. So were his friends. The town of Trinidad, Colorado, where they came from, was a crossroads for railroad passengers, ranchers, and miners. All of them had money. Harvey and his buddies helped themselves to some money from all of those folks.

Harvey would still be in Trinidad, stealing money and staying one jump ahead of the law, if his uncles hadn't offered him a chance to bring in a little more cash for his efforts. He knew his buddies would jump at the chance of joining him.

His Uncle Bryce Castle had told him to take the train from Durango, and he wasn't arguing about that. The train had gone through more towns than he knew existed in Colorado, but it had taken only three days instead of two weeks. Besides that, he hadn't had to worry about the Utes or Jicarilla Apache taking his scalp along the way.

As the train rolled to a stop in Trinidad, Harvey had no doubt about where his first stop needed to be. The Lilly Belle Saloon was where he would find his gang. If they weren't drinking, they were sure to be gambling.

He found them at the bar, drinking beer. That told him a lot. If they had any money, they would have been at the gambling tables, drinking whiskey. Harvey had no time to waste, so he called them over to a table. One hour and a bottle of whiskey later, all three were ready to join him on the trip to Pueblo.

The brothers Clyde and Jesse were Harvey's oldest friends. They let him do the planning and they did whatever he asked them to do. They didn't mind using their guns to get what the gang needed. That suited Harvey just fine. The third man, Henry, went by the nickname Ox. His sheer size and strength made him useful. Many vaults had been opened after a threat from Ox.

After the first bottle of whiskey was empty, Harvey ordered a second and explained how they were going to rob the First National Bank of Pueblo. All three blinked a time or two before nodding. They had never operated outside of Trinidad before, but then again, they were broke, and Harvey had a plan.

They left the saloon and took the train to Pueblo. Riding a train was something else that Clyde, Jesse, and Ox had never done. Harvey's uncles needed this done fast, so they had supplied the money for train rides to Pueblo and Leadville. Harvey planned to spend his uncles' money for the train trip to Leadville, but he expected to have plenty more cash in his pockets by then.

On the train, Harvey huddled with his crew and told them what they would each be doing. They would watch the bank for a day or so and decide on the best time to strike. Then, all four would move in. Clyde would watch the door and street, letting them know if they had to leave suddenly. Jesse would take the money from the cages. Harvey and Ox would get the vault opened and empty it out.

Harvey had decided to skip the part where somebody created a distraction, like the way he had started a fire in the hay wagon in Leadville. It had seemed like a waste of time to him, and he felt he needed all four of his men at the bank.

His three friends asked no questions at all. Half an hour after he had told them what they would be doing, all three were asleep. Harvey stared out the train window and wondered how rich he would be after the two robberies.

I was sitting up long after Joanna had gone to bed. Little Ethan had been asleep for hours now. I couldn't seem to shut down my brain and go to sleep. I stared at the fire I had going in the fireplace, trying to think about what else I could do to get on top of things.

I had almost the western half of Colorado to worry about, and there were some great targets for outlaws in most of that territory. I had made a start on figuring out who a couple of these guys might be, and had the posters on them, but there were more bandits out there. The toughest problem to solve, though, might be where they would strike next.

If I didn't even know where they were going to show up, how could I get there in time to stop a robbery? Even with the railroads to help me get there, along with Hardison and his militia, it would likely be too late to stop them. Those guys could use the railroads too, I reminded myself. That's why I wanted the Pinkerton detectives to have those posters.

I thought about how they had struck here in Silverton. I had seen that guy with the deep scar on his cheek before the robbery. It had actually been several days before the robbery. He'd been looking things over ahead of time. If only I had known about him when I saw him the first time. I needed somebody on the spot in these places, watching for me.

That's when I sat straight up in my chair and swung my head to look at the posters lying on the floor beside me. That could help! What if somebody who lived in some of these towns had a poster and was watching for those faces when they first came to town to look things over? They could send a telegram to give me a head start!

I picked up the list from the floor beside me of possible places the outlaws could hit. I ran my finger up and down the town names. Two of them jumped out at me: Leadville, because of all the mining money, and Durango, because it was a railroad hub.

A grin spread slowly across my face. I knew people in both of these towns who could help me. I had been in Leadville for several weeks just a couple of years ago. A man who had worked for me, Mal White, had come along to help restore the law in Leadville. Mal got a chance to buy a saloon there and I'd heard he was doing great. What was the name of that saloon... *The Rusty Bucket*!

I pulled one copy of each poster and set it aside. I would get Carlton Boone at Pinkerton's to send the copies to Leadville by train. I started smiling again. What better place to have someone watching for me than in the best saloon in town?

That left Durango. I had started out in Durango when I'd first come back to Colorado. Holt and I had started out by working for the railroad. Joanna had come with us to Durango. She had taken a job at the bakery.

The bakery! I sat straight up in the chair again. Joanna had worked at a place called *Ma's Bakery*. It was at least as popular with the miners and railroad workers as the saloons. Ma was a good friend to us. She would definitely help me.

I put two more posters in the pile to send to Carlton Boone, and I would make sure Mal and Ma both knew how to get a telegram to me. I stood and stretched, then put out the fire. I was feeling better about things. Maybe I could get to sleep now.

Harvey and Clyde watched the First National Bank of Pueblo from a café across Union Street. It was their second morning to watch. Midday yesterday, they had moved from the café to a saloon two shops down the street.

At exactly eight o'clock, a man rode up and entered the bank, pulling out a large set of keys and selecting one for the door. Like yesterday, the man wore a charcoal three-piece suit with a starched white collar and necktie. His lace-up black boots were shining just as much as they had been yesterday. The bowler hat on his head looked like the same hat he'd worn the day before.

"Same guy, ain't it?" Clyde muttered. He took a long, loud slurp of his coffee and waved for a refill.

"Yup," was the only answer he got from Harvey.

"Gotta be the president," Clyde offered. He got no answer at all this time.

Clyde waited for his refill, then decided to take a chance. He would ask Harvey to reconsider his plan. The one he was thinking about looked easy. Harvey's way seemed like a lot of work.

"You thinkin' what I'm thinkin'?" asked Clyde. He braced himself for the answer. They all knew about Harvey's temper.

To Clyde's surprise, Harvey seemed to think things over. "Yeah, mebbe," he finally mumbled.

Harvey watched until the man disappeared inside the bank, then turned back to his breakfast. "Ain't nobody else over there, he's all by hisself," Harvey said, spraying toast crumbs across the table.

Clyde ignored the toast crumbs and waited for Harvey to continue. "Wouldn't have to watch nobody else, jest one guy on the door and one guy watchin' horses. Ox and me would make him open the vault."

Harvey looked around the café. "The sheriff didn't come in here till nine o'clock yestiddy," he said, half to himself. "We could empty that vault and be clean outta town by then."

Clyde left off slurping his coffee and waited for more. Harvey picked up his spoon and stirred his own coffee. "What's the nearest rail station to here?" he asked Clyde. "We couldn't rob the bank and get on the train here in town. We got to go somewhere else to catch a train to Leadville."

Clyde furrowed his brow and thought. "North of here, a town called Fountain," he said. "'Bout a day's ride, I'd say. Ain't much there except the train station, but we could catch a train there."

Harvey nodded and took a sip of coffee. He made a face and set the cup down. "It's cold," he announced. He waved at the waitress for a refill, then glanced at a clock in the corner. "Let's wait and see when the sheriff shows hisself," he decided. "If he ain't out and around to the café before nine, we'll go surprise that banker over there at eight o'clock tomorrow morning."

———

Harvey wasn't quite sure what time it was right now, but he had left the café just a few minutes before eight o'clock. This made the third morning they had been in Pueblo. Sitting on a bench across the street from the bank, he muttered curses under his breath as Union Street started coming to life for a new day. Riders and carriages were moving up and down the street. He was sure it was at least eight thirty, and the bank president hadn't come in yet.

Harvey glanced across the street, where Clyde pretended to check his horse's hooves. Looking to his left, he saw Ox and Jessie on another bench. Jessie had leaned back and pushed his hat down over his nose, pretending to sleep. Ox was too big to ignore, no matter what he was doing.

Harvey's head snapped back to watch as a woman crossed Union Street toward the bank. She reached into her bag and pulled out a ring of keys. By the time she had inserted a key into the lock on the bank's front door, Harvey was already trotting across the street.

Clyde stared, mouthing the word *teller*. Harvey didn't care what her job was. He had waited long enough. As the teller turned to push the door shut behind her, Harvey shoved her backward, jumped into the bank, and waved Clyde inside. He was followed by Ox. Jessie stayed outside, bringing their horses down to hitch them to the rail in front of the bank.

Harvey advanced on the woman threateningly. The color drained from her face. "I'm just a teller," she murmured.

Harvey leaned over her, his nose inches from hers. "Where is the president? That guy in the Sunday-go-to-meetin' clothes that's here every mornin'?"

"Mr. Stinson," she nodded, her voice barely loud enough to hear. "He's the president. He walked over to my house to tell me he is sick today. He won't be here."

Harvey's fists clenched and unclenched in frustration. He gave the woman a shove. "Open the vault," he yelled.

Her head shook back and forth. "I c...can't," she quavered. "I don't know the combination. Only Mr. Stinson." She collapsed back against the wall.

"Ox!" Harvey waved at the towering man standing at the entrance. "Git over here."

Ox stepped forward slowly, staring at the woman, who had slid to the floor. She was sobbing quietly.

Ox shook his head and stared at Harvey. "I ain't gonna hurt no woman," he growled. He walked back over and stood against the wall.

Harvey cursed and leaned over to yank the woman to her feet. He pulled down his bandana to make sure she could hear him. "What can you open?" he hissed.

The teller pointed at the cages. "I can open the cages," she whispered, avoiding those threatening eyes. "All the cages. I can open them."

"Do it!". Harvey waited until she finished, then shoved her to the floor. "Clyde!" he bellowed. "Git over here with a sack!"

They were done within minutes. Harvey stared at the small pile of coins at the bottom of the sack. He swore, then shoved the last cage over onto the floor. It made a surprisingly loud clatter when it landed. Not finished, he grabbed a sculpted ceramic bowl decorating the table at the bank's entrance. He threw it against the wall, where it shattered.

Clyde and Ox gathered at the front entrance, staring nervously out the window and waiting for Harvey to call it off.

Hal Oberman was hustling down the street to open the general store. He had slept late that morning, like he did about half the time. He was relieved when he reached Union Street and saw no one waiting outside the store. He slowed his pace while he fished in his pocket for the keys.

As he prepared to step up to the boardwalk, Hal noticed a lot of horses tied up in front of the bank next door. Four horses, he thought—that was a lot of customers when the bank wasn't even open yet. His eyes roved over to the porch, where he saw one man lounging against the wall of the bank.

Just as he stepped up to the boardwalk, he heard a loud crash next door, followed by another. The man in front of the bank came off the wall. Hal saw the man's hand drop toward his gun belt.

Hal turned and walked away, crossing the street and moving toward the café. He knew he could find the sheriff having himself a coffee in there at this hour. He stepped inside and spotted Sheriff Sexton immediately. Hal dropped into the chair across the table.

"I think somebody is robbing the bank," Hal said

in low tones. He went on to describe what he had seen.

Sexton rose immediately. He needed his Winchester, and that was in the sheriff's office. He left the café and turned left, moving away from the bank. He wouldn't even think about facing outlaws at the bank without that Winchester. Hal Oberman trotted along beside him. He was the only deputy Sexton would have today.

———

Sheriff Sexton handed one rifle to Oberman and told him to take up a position to the south on Union Street, behind a stack of wood next to the feed store. "Take the back alley to get there," Sexton told him. "Keep your head down. Take a shot if you've got one."

Sexton thought it was likely they would ride north, where they could get out of town sooner. Sexton took the back alley to the north and took up a position behind the water trough at the edge of town. He would give them one warning shot, he decided. After that, he meant business.

He heard them coming before he saw them. As they came around a bend in Union Street, all four of them were in his sights. Sexton raised his sights slightly, fired one shot, then dove behind the water trough. An answering round of bullets slammed into the trough.

Sexton crawled to the other end of the water trough, hearing another bullet or two slam into the trough opposite where he had just been. Sucking in his breath, Sexton rose and fired at the nearest horseman. He saw the man grab his shoulder and duck.

Sexton dove again as another volley of bullets came his way. He stayed down as he heard the thunder of hooves dying away. When he came out from behind the water trough, the street was quiet. He walked to the street and saw a few drops of blood in the dust. At least he had hit one of them.

Sexton turned and trotted toward the bank. Hal Oberman emerged from the lumber pile next to the feed store. They reached the doors of the bank together. Sexton pulled his Colt, and they rushed through the door. He swept the pistol from side to side, but they saw only the teller, Mrs. Watson, sobbing quietly on the floor.

TWELVE
ON TO LEADVILLE

S heriff Sexton sent word for Stinson, the bank president, to come in to assess how much money had been taken this morning. Stinson arrived in a hurry and promised to stay at the bank until he had a dollar total from the three cages. He hung a Closed sign on the door, pulled a set of books from his desk, and got to work.

Sexton decided the teller, Mrs. Watson, might do better if he took her away from the holdup scene and moved her to the sheriff's office. Once there, she accepted a brandy to calm her nerves and began responding to Sexton's questions about the robbery.

She said a man had appeared at the door and pushed her inside as soon as she unlocked the bank. Two more came behind him. It was that first man who had really taken charge of the whole thing. He had pushed her down and threatened her when she said she couldn't open the vault.

She remembered how the first man had called over a huge man standing in the back. He had refused to hurt her when she said she couldn't open the vault. Mrs. Watson was very clear on that. The big man had left her alone. The first man had then forced her to open the cages and pushed her to the ground while he took the money.

There had been a loud crashing noise in front after they emptied the cages, then she heard no more sounds in the bank. She had kept her head down long after she heard them leave. There had been gunshots, then the sheriff had come in.

Sheriff Sexton sat back and let her finish the brandy. He could think of only two questions for the teller.

"Did you get a look at any of them?" he asked.

She shook her head, then stopped and set the brandy down.

"Well, the mean one—the first one that took the money. He pulled his mask down and got his face very close to mine when he threatened me. He was a very young man. He had a…rather prominent nose. Light-colored eyebrows. I think he is blonde-headed."

Sexton pulled a pencil and paper from his pocket and took some notes. "Color of his eyes?"

She shrugged. "I'm not really sure. Maybe blue."

"Get a look at any of the others?"

She shook her head. "That one in the back was a very big man, but I didn't get a look at his face. They wore bandanas over their faces."

Sexton nodded. "Just one more question, Mrs.

Watson. Did you hear any names? Did they talk to each other and use names?"

She leaned back thoughtfully and stared out the window. Suddenly, she leaned forward. "Clyde!" she said. "The mean one with the large nose called the other one Clyde. Not the big one, the third man."

Sexton stood and extended a hand. "Thank you, Mrs. Watson. I'm going to walk you home now. I'll have one of the ladies in town check in on you after a while."

The sheriff walked to the bank after dropping Mrs. Watson at her house. Stinson told him the robbers had gotten only fifty-three dollars this morning. Sexton jotted down the number, shook his head, and walked to the telegraph station. They had gotten little money, and nobody had been hurt, but the marshal for this district needed to know. That's about all he could do. This bunch didn't rate a posse chase.

Sexton got a message pad at the telegraph office and took his time, telling Brad Anderson how much money had been taken. There were four men, including one who stayed outside, according to the only witness. He described the man with the large nose and blonde hair, the big man, and the one named Clyde.

Sexton picked up the telegram, handed it to the clerk, then took it back. He added a note to say he believed he had shot one of them in the shoulder.

Anderson should be on the lookout for a wounded man in this gang.

He rechecked the telegram, gave it back to the clerk to send, and then went back over to check on things at the bank.

━━━

They weren't making much progress toward the town of Fountain. Harvey turned to yell at the other three from time to time, but Jesse was bent over the saddle, holding on to his shoulder and moaning.

"Gotta stop for Jesse!" Clyde was helping his brother down from the saddle. Ox was holding the horse and watching the backtrail.

"Can't stop!" Harvey bellowed, wheeling his horse around and galloping back to the others. Nobody was listening. Clyde was peeling Jesse's shirt away from his left shoulder. Ox had tethered the horses, grabbed his Winchester, and taken up watch over the backtrail.

Harvey cursed under his breath, but resigned himself to a stop. Without these guys, he didn't have a gang for Leadville. He didn't want to think about what his uncles would do if he failed in Leadville. He especially didn't want to think about what Warner would do. He'd heard things about Warner. Things that scared him.

Harvey kneeled beside the saddle blanket where Jesse was biting down on a rag from his saddlebag. Clyde had pulled the shirt back to expose a raw, open wound where the bullet had grazed his brother's shoulder. Clyde rose, went to his saddlebag, and came back with another rag and a bottle of whiskey.

"This is gonna hurt," he mumbled.

Jesse bit down on the rag and writhed as Clyde splashed whiskey on the wound. He relaxed and mumbled to himself as Clyde rose again, pulled a knife from his belt, and walked toward a stand of trees.

"Where you goin'?" Harvey barked.

Clyde began scraping at a tree. "Pine tar." He began wiping his knife on the rag he had taken from his saddlebag. "Gotta keep this rag from stickin' to the wound when we take it off."

Clyde returned and wrapped the rag around Jesse's shoulder. Jesse, Harvey noticed, mercifully seemed to have passed out.

"Gotta camp here," Clyde announced.

Harvey opened his mouth to protest, then changed his mind. He needed this crew. By the time they got to Leadville, he would find a way to let them know he was in charge again.

Ox moved away from his lookout position and began gathering firewood. They didn't have much food, but maybe they could shoot a deer. There had been no sign of pursuit by a posse. Harvey laughed bitterly to himself. He had counted the money they got this morning. No wonder they didn't have anybody chasing them. He shouldered his rifle and went out to scout for a deer.

I sat in the doc's office while he patched up Holt and changed his bandage one more time. I knew Holt was feeling better because he complained the whole time. Doc shook his head, rolled his eyes, and put up with it.

"You take him," Doc finally said. "He's like a grizzly with a sore tooth. Maybe if you take him down to your saloon and put a whiskey in him, he'll make fit company for somebody."

I held the door open for Holt and grinned at Doc. "You come down there too. I'll give you a free whiskey or two for puttin' up with him."

I hustled Holt out the door before he could get up a head of steam, complaining about the free drinks. He brightened up when we went to the *Suds 'n Such* and I fixed him up with a comfortable chair behind the bar.

I showed him a telegram I had picked up this morning from Brad Anderson. He told me he was passing along what he'd been told by the sheriff in Pueblo. They'd had a robbery at the bank, but it didn't sound like the robbers got much.

Holt read the telegram and passed it back. "Whaddya think?" he asked.

The kid working the bar brought me a beer and I sucked about half of it down while I thought about it. "I don't know if it's the same gang or not," I admitted. I looked at the telegram again. "They sure didn't get much money. That bunch that came here to Silverton knew what they were doing."

I looked over at Holt. "You didn't get much of a look at anybody, did you?"

Holt shook his head. "Bandanas all around covering their faces, and they were in a hurry." He touched his shoulder gingerly. "One of 'em was a pretty good shot, too. Nope, I didn't really see anybody."

I looked at the telegram again. "Nobody here saw a really big guy, like they described in Pueblo. He's new for sure. That one guy, though...the tall kid with the big nose...he might be the same."

Holt looked puzzled. "Two gangs with some of the same guys?"

"Maybe." I tucked the telegram into my pocket. "The main thing is, where are they gonna show up next? They won't quit after they only got fifty-three dollars in Pueblo." I got up and headed for the door.

"Where you goin'?"

"To the train station," I said. "I want to see where a couple quick train trips from somewhere close to Pueblo could take them."

━━

Half an hour later, I was still staring at a railroad map and thinking things over. You could get to lots of towns these days on trains leaving Pueblo. Denver was a direct line, taking maybe only six to eight hours. I couldn't see them going to Denver, though. The governor was doing his best to make sure Denver was a safe place. They could go south, but that would take them away from the richer mining towns.

Out of the places I thought most likely, that left Durango and Leadville. You could get to Durango by train, but it would take a while, maybe two days. There were several stops along the way.

The train to Leadville would pass through Royal Gorge and make a stop, but you could get there in about twelve hours. That one looked more likely to me. It was closer, and there was a lot of mining money flowing into Leadville.

I stopped at the telegraph office and sent a telegram to Captain Anderson, telling him to take his squad of militia to Leadville. I told him to look out for a young blonde kid with a big nose, somebody named Clyde, or maybe a giant of a kid keeping company with those other two.

Myself, I planned to make Durango my first trip as a marshal. I would take some of these posters with me, go to see Ma at the bakery, and look the town over. Maybe one of those guys who hadn't been in on the Pueblo robbery was doing the same right now.

━━━

Harvey faced Clyde across the small clearing where they had made camp. Jessie was on his bedroll at the edge of the clearing, sweat pouring down his face, leaning back against his saddle. Ox kneeled next to Jessie, ready to shield him from gunfire.

It had come to that. Harvey had informed them that Jessie had to move this morning or be left behind. Jessie had made one effort to rise. He had fallen and passed out, then Clyde had announced he was staying with Jessie. Ox said he was staying, too.

A part of Harvey's brain was telling him he would have to kill both Clyde and Ox if he didn't back down. The rest of his brain was telling him that the gang would never look at him as the leader again if he did back down. Now he didn't know what to do.

Seconds passed. Harvey's eyes flicked back and forth from Clyde to Ox. Clyde's eyes never wavered. He was locked in on Harvey. It was Ox who finally broke the standoff. He rose and walked quietly across the clearing, then laid a massive paw on Harvey's shoulder.

"One more day. I think he can move in one more day." He pointed at Clyde, then Jessie. "We stay together. All of us got to stay together."

Harvey slowly relaxed and turned away. "Tomorrow," he said over his shoulder. "We'll see if Jessie can get on his horse tomorrow."

Harvey didn't know it, but the delay had saved his hide. Pinkerton had flooded the trains leaving Pueblo with agents yesterday and this morning, looking for the blonde kid with the hook nose. By tomorrow, they would spread out in all directions and get on the trains that had come in from Pueblo since the robbery. Pinkertons hadn't expected this delay. Now Harvey and his crew could get to Leadville without seeing one of their agents on the train.

Harvey, Clyde, and Ox looked through the train window nervously as they wound along the Arkansas River Valley and started the final climb into Leadville. They were used to the elevation at Trinidad, a town that sat at six thousand feet, but Leadville was at ten thousand feet. There were places where the tracks just seemed to hang off the side of the mountain.

Jessie braced himself against the back seat of the coach, wincing when the train took a curve or hit a rough spot in the tracks. He had a coat lying over his injured shoulder and he kept his eyes closed.

The train leveled out on a high plateau as they rolled into Leadville. With a hiss and a shriek of metal, the D & RG engine came to a stop. The four outlaws stood and stepped down from the coach. They formed a shield around Jesse to keep him from being jostled by the crowd and pushed through the knots of people waiting on the platform.

The four of them spread out after collecting their horses and putting them into a livery stable. Harvey assigned the jobs. Jesse would get them a couple rooms at a boardinghouse and scout the saloons. They all knew that Jesse could use a stiff drink, and sometimes a man could gather some interesting news at a saloon.

Clyde would watch the silver smelters. Silver ore was pouring into town when the miners came in. The smelters used heat and blast furnaces to separate the silver from iron, copper, and whatever other metals were in the ore, leaving purified silver. This town ran on silver. The workers came and left from the smelters in shifts. Harvey and the gang needed to know when those shifts of workers might arrive at the bank with their pay. They needed a quiet, empty bank when they struck.

Harvey and Ox had the job of watching the bank, a squat building that sat at the corner of Seventh Street and Harrison. They needed to know the slowest times of day at this bank, and they needed to get an idea about the workers, the guards, if any, and the vault. They all had three days to learn what they could about Leadville and then make their final plans.

Clyde stopped at the first saloon he saw to find out how many smelters there were in Leadville. When he found out there were five smelters in Leadville, Clyde spread a few beers around to find out what the shift hours were. After all, Harvey really only needed to know when the smelter workers might show up at the bank.

After visiting three saloons over the next day and a half, Clyde confidently reported to Harvey that all five smelters had twelve-hour shifts from six o'clock to six o'clock—one morning shift and one night shift. Workers were likely to show up at the bank early in the morning or late in the afternoon.

━━━

Jesse went to a boardinghouse on Seventh Street and booked two rooms. He would bunk in with his brother Clyde, and Harvey and Ox would share the other. After sleeping for several hours, he felt better and left in search of some food and some whiskey. After all, his job was going to saloons and getting information. Finding out about the local law was the first thing he needed to do.

After a steak at the café, Jesse stopped outside a saloon just down the street and read the name above the door: *The Rusty Bucket*. He stepped inside and up to the bar. The barkeep walked over and stuck out a hand.

"Mal White," he said. "I own this place."

Jesse nodded and mumbled a name he'd last used about ten years ago. After watching the barkeep step over to serve another customer, he ordered a second whiskey and tried to ask his questions without making the barkeep suspicious.

"I used to know the sheriff around here," he said, laying a gold coin on the counter to pay. "His name was…Hodges, I think."

The barkeep wiped a glass dry and shook his head. "We ain't had a sheriff by that name since I've been here." He reached for another glass. "Sheriff's name is Thomas these days."

"Huh." Jesse winced a little as he leaned forward on the bar to grab the whiskey glass. "Mebbe I'm thinkin' of the deputy."

The barkeep shook his head. "Ain't got no deputy right now. Maybe they're lookin' for one. Not sure."

Jesse nodded and took his whiskey to a table at the side of the room. He'd learned a few things he needed to know. He would keep his head down for the rest of the night.

———

Behind the bar, Mal White pulled out the poster he'd been given by a Pinkerton man yesterday, along with a telegram from his friend Latigo Smith. He looked at the poster, then at the stranger who had just left the bar to take a seat at a table. He shook his head. They weren't the same man. Still, those were some strange questions to be asking first thing when you met somebody.

Fifteen minutes later, Mal told one of his employees to cover him at the bar. He trotted down to the telegraph office and fired off a telegram to Latigo Smith. Back at the saloon, a young blonde man who might well fit the poster he had put under the bar had just joined the man with all the questions at his table.

THIRTEEN
DEAD IN SHANTYTOWN

The first telegram from Mal White lay on the bar beside me, and now I was thinking about his response to my follow-up telegram. The first one told me Mal had seen the kid who'd been in on the Pueblo robbery and had probably held the horses for the Silverton holdup, too.

I'd sent him a telegram to ask about the man with the deep scar on one cheek. His answer told me he hadn't seen the man with the deep scar on his cheek. His description of the second man he'd seen at *The Rusty Bucket*, talking with the holdup kid, didn't sound like anybody I'd heard about yet.

Holt saw me muttering to myself and scratching my head, so he brought a beer and plunked it down on the bar with his good arm. "Where are ya at with this holdup stuff, pard?"

I took a pull at the beer and mumbled at myself for a while. "Not sure," I admitted. "This same holdup gang is at work, but maybe they've split up. Sounds like they're looking things over in Leadville, but maybe not all of 'em."

I had ordered Captain Hardison to take his whole squad of ten militiamen to Leadville. I moved my beer glass around in circles on the bar top and wondered if I should have him send five of them down to me.

I decided to leave 'em all up there. I didn't even know where the rest of these guys were or how many of them were out there planning something else. I only knew that the guy with the scar hadn't shown up in Leadville.

Holt left me alone while I did some more muttering and head scratching. I remembered four banks in Leadville when I had been there with Brad Anderson a couple years ago. The biggest by far was *The First National Bank of Leadville*. They did most of the business with the silver miners in the area.

I had to let Hardison run his own squad up there. He and his men should arrive by train in the morning. I decided to have a telegram waiting for him when he got there. I would tell him to concentrate on the big bank. He could keep an eye on the other three with just a few men.

I hopped off the stool, waved goodbye to Holt, and walked over to the telegraph office. After that, I would go back to the ranch for the rest of the day, then take the train to Durango tomorrow.

It had taken the best part of a day to ride from their hideout to Durango. Matt Warner was just now cooling off. Early this morning, he'd been squared off for a fistfight or gunfight with Bryce Castle. Warner hadn't really cared which kind of fight they would have.

Castle wanted nobody to leave their hideout on a mesa south of Silverton. Warner was not only sick and tired of being holed up with the Castle brothers, but they were also running out of provisions. Deer meat three times a day wasn't Warner's idea of what he wanted to eat for the next two weeks.

Warner had announced he would be going into Durango, and Bryce Castle had told him he couldn't go. Bryce was worried about Warner's scar being recognized.

They had squared off over the morning campfire, and Warner had made it clear he didn't care whether he fought with his fists or his guns. Castle took a long look at the Colt on Warner's hip and backed off.

Warner had brought Tom Castle's horse with him to use as a packhorse, and now he loaded up the horses with some provisions at the general store. He had no intention of sleeping in town at a boarding-house, and he knew he might be recognized in a saloon.

Not ready to turn around and start on the trail home, Warner took a look around town for anything that might put him in a better mood for sleeping under the stars and taking another full day's ride tomorrow to get back to the mesa.

He walked past a newspaper vendor's stand. He glanced at a paper called *The Durango Herald*. A head-line caught his attention as he walked past. He stopped and bought a newspaper. The headline read *Bank Robbery in Pueblo.*

Warner scanned the article, shook his head in disgust, then crossed the street to stuff the paper in his saddlebag. He turned and glanced down the street, where a sign caught his eye. The sign said *Ma's Bakery.*

Warner bought himself a slice of apple pie and liked it so much he bought an entire pie and a loaf of bread for his return trip. He had no intention of sharing any of it. He would eat it all before he got back to the hideout.

Leaving the bakery, Warner didn't see the white-haired lady behind the counter slip out a poster on the shelf under the counter to check the picture. The scar on the right side of that face, she thought, was unmistakable.

Warner rode out through the north side of town just as twilight was setting in. He rode past the shanty-town at the edge of town, where newly arrived miners and those hoping to find work were living in tents. It was a rough crowd, but Warner paid no attention as he rode through.

A few hundred yards past the shantytown, two men emerged from the bushes at the side of the trail, holding shotguns loosely aimed at Warner. He rode a little closer, then reined in his horse and stared at the two men.

One of them snickered and spat on the trail. "Git off," he snarled. "We're gonna take what we want, then you kin ride on." He motioned with the shotgun. "Git yer hands up where I kin see 'em."

Warner left his right hand resting on his thigh. He

nodded at the empty trail behind the two robbers. "Sure," he said easily, "but what are you boys gonna do about him?"

They fell for his trick just long enough to take a half-turn and leave the shotgun barrels pointing at the side of the road. That was plenty of time for Warner. He palmed the Colt and fired only twice. Both men fell at the side of the trail, shot through the heart. Warner shook his head and rode between the two dead bodies on his way out of town.

I had telegraphed to let a sheriff know in Durango, named Carnes, that I would be coming in on the one p.m. train, but I didn't expect him to meet at the station. I stepped down from the coach and saw a man with a badge approaching me. He pointed at the badge I was wearing, then at himself.

"Sheriff Carnes," he said, "glad you're here today, Marshal."

We walked down to claim my horse, and it didn't take him long to fill me in on what had just happened in Durango.

"Two dead men, out in the miner's shantytown," he told me. "I just found out about it this morning." He shook his head. "I think they were shot last night, but nobody came down to tell me until some kid showed up at my office a few hours ago."

We walked my horse down to the sheriff's office, where I tethered him to the rail. He offered me a cup of coffee when we went inside. I had my doubts, but I took it. It actually wasn't bad. I had a second cup.

"Have you been able to go out there and look it over?"

He nodded. "Went out there a few hours ago. Two guys, both of 'em just got here a few days ago, that's what they say. Looks like they braced the wrong man with shotguns and both of 'em took one bullet in the heart each." He shook his head. "That was some fancy shootin'. Don't know how he got the drop on two shotguns."

I put down my coffee cup and turned that one over in my head a couple times. "Could anybody tell you anything more?"

Carnes shrugged. "One guy at shantytown told me he was leadin' a packhorse. Kinda loaded down, he said." Carnes shrugged again. "I went down to the general store. The owner said he sold some supplies to a stranger yesterday evening, but says he's got no description at all. Just a reglar guy, that's what he said."

"Hmmm." I tugged at my mustache, which is what Joanna says I do when I'm thinkin' hard. I picked up my hat and stood. "How about if we go and have a look in shantytown?" I said. "I guess you've tried following his tracks? Two horses and all?"

"I tried," he said. "Follered 'em for about a mile but lost him there. Looks like he mebbe scrambled them hosses across some bare rock face and then walked 'em in a stream."

I grabbed Buck's reins and mounted up, then I heard a voice calling me. "Latigo! Latigo Smith!"

It was Ma from the bakery. I swung back down and let her squash me in a big hug. She stood back and inspected me. "Ain't you a sight! You look like you could use a piece of pie."

She grabbed my arm and steered me toward the bakery. "You too, Sheriff," she called over her shoulder. I noticed Carnes didn't object. He trotted along behind us to the bakery.

"How's Joanna?" she asked. "I heard you've got a young 'un now!"

I filled her in on things while she brought two massive pieces of pie and settled down at the table with us. She waited until our plates were clean, then dropped a poster in front of me. It was the man with the scar.

My eyebrows climbed halfway up my forehead, and I stared at Ma.

"He was here," she said. "Yesterday. I sent you a telegram, but it prob'ly didn't catch up with you yet, what with you comin' down here."

"Here in the bakery? Anybody with him?"

She shook her head. "He bought a piece of pie, then bought a whole pie and a loaf of bread. All by himself. He stuffed the food in his saddlebag and rode off."

I looked at Carnes. "Let's look out there at shanty-town," I said.

I turned around to say goodbye to Ma. "Anything else you can tell me?"

She shrugged. "About your size, I'd say, pretty big

man. Red checkered shirt, black pants, black hat. Wore a gun like he knew what to do with it. Hardly said a word while he was in here."

She gave me a hug and walked me out. "You come back here before you go."

━━━

I rode out to shantytown with Carnes, and he took me to where he had found the bodies. They were gone, of course, but he showed me the place where he had found the bodies and described the scene.

I walked around checking for boot prints and looking in the brush near the trail. There wasn't much to see. Carnes had questioned people in the tents near this place, but nobody claimed to have heard or seen anything. I knew that likely meant they were just scared.

We followed the tracks leading away from the double killing. It was two days later, but not many people had ridden through here, and I could still see the tracks of a man on horseback leading another.

A mile down the trail, I could see exactly what Carnes had been talking about. The tracks disappeared into a deep, swift-moving stream. There were many stretches with bare rock rising out of the stream, and I could see several places out ahead of me where a man could lie in wait and drygulch anybody foolish enough to pursue him.

I called off the tracking and rode back into town. When we reached Main Street, Carnes moved his horse up alongside mine.

"Whaddya think?"

"I think he'll be back," I said. "These guys have a way of checkin' out the town before they strike. We need to be watching for them."

Another thought hit me about how this gang had operated before. I told Carnes, then rode over to the telegraph office to tell Captain Hardison in Leadville. If there's an explosion or a fire, I told him, they're likely about to strike, but they'll do it somewhere else. Don't waste much time checking out the fire or explosion.

I sent the telegram, then went to check into a hotel. I had a feeling about this. I was going to stay for a few days in Durango.

━━━

Ox shoved the hay wagon into a spot directly across the street from the Silver Bow Bank in Leadville. He had left the wagon here last night and had put his horse back into a livery stable. He didn't mind pushing the wagon himself to get it a little closer to the bank. His horse was tethered a few blocks down the street this morning.

Ox liked the assignment he'd been given for today's robbery. All he had to do was light the hay on fire, yell "FIRE!" at the top of his lungs, then skedaddle over to the First National Bank. Harvey, Clyde, and Jessie should have finished robbing the bank by then. All Ox had to do was ride out of town with them.

Ox looked both ways, then pulled two matches out

of his shirt pocket. He scraped them on the bed of the wagon, tossed them into the hay, and stood back. When the flames started leaping up, he yelled "Fire!" and trotted toward his horse.

Ox had taken only five steps when two militiamen stepped away from a shopfront and aimed their rifles squarely at his chest. Ox looked back and forth at the two gun barrels, then slowly raised his hands into the air.

▭

Harvey couldn't believe how well this was going. They had hit the bank at exactly nine o'clock, and there was only one customer in the whole place. That customer and the three tellers laid on the ground, just like they were told, and Clyde was almost through emptying the money from the cages into his burlap bag.

Harvey swung a glance toward the front door. Jessie was bracing himself against a desk near the door, but he was watching the street and watching the horses. He would holler if anybody showed up at the door. Harvey grinned to himself. By now, Ox had set fire to a hay wagon outside another bank. That would keep the shcriff busy.

Harvey trotted over to a plump, pink-cheeked man sitting behind the biggest desk in the place.

"You the owner?" he growled.

The man shook his head. His answer came out as a high-pitched squeak. "No, but I'm the president. What do you want?"

Harvey waved his pistol at the vault at the back. "Open that up!" he barked.

The man nodded slowly and got heavily to his feet. He plodded toward the vault. Harvey prodded him with the pistol every few steps to keep him moving.

Stopping in front of the dial, he spun it back and forth a few times while Harvey watched closely. He stopped after the third spin and reached for the handle. Harvey couldn't believe his luck when the door creaked open.

"On the floor! Hands on your head!" he commanded. The bank president did so.

Harvey stepped into the vault, and the grin spread across his face again. He went for the gold bars first, then started scooping silver coins and processed silver ore into his bag. He stepped over the bank president and barked another command through the vault door.

"Clyde! Git in here and help!"

Clyde trotted into the vault and sucked in a deep breath while he looked around. He stepped over to some piles of cash and scooped those into his bag. Harvey tossed a few gold bars into Clyde's bag to lighten his own load, then took another look around the vault.

"The rest of this ain't worth it," he decided. "Let's light a shuck and get outta here!"

They moved back through the bank. Harvey growled to the employees and customers to stay on the floor. They joined Jessie at the door. He was watching through the window.

"Ain't seen nuthin' out there," he breathed.

Harvey yanked the door open and charged

through. He reached the edge of the boardwalk and had reached out to unhitch his horse when he realized that somebody had yelled at him.

"Hold it right there!"

He stared across the street, and Clyde and Jessie screeched to a stop beside him. Now, Harvey could see a dark blue uniform across the street, then another one beside the first one. Two men had stepped out of the alley across the street!

Three more uniforms stepped out of the next alley to the right, but Harvey didn't see them. His gun was still in his hand, right where it had been when he had stepped out of the bank. His reaction was pure instinct. He let out a snarl of rage and lifted his gun to take aim at one of those blue uniforms.

He felt a heavy blow in his chest before his ears registered the roar of gunfire.

FOURTEEN
WATCHING AND WAITING

aptain Hardison didn't have time to send his squad to get some breakfast after their train rolled into Leadville. The newly elected sheriff in town met the train at the station and stepped up to inform Hardison he had just received a telegram. He handed the message to Hardison and stepped back while Hardison read it.

Hardison, wondering if the sheriff had already read his telegram, opened it and read Lat Smith's instructions to cover all four banks in Leadville, and to pay little attention to any fire or minor explosion that might be a diversionary tactic. Smith advised him to pay special attention to the First National Bank.

Hardison folded the telegram and stuffed it into his jacket pocket.

"Sheriff," he said, "I am taking four of my men to The First National Bank of Leadville immediately. Would you take my five remaining men to the other three banks in town? If you would join them, that would give us two men guarding each bank."

The Leadville sheriff nodded and waited while Hardison separated his men. The sheriff left with the five assigned to him, but first stopped briefly to give Hardison directions to the First National.

Hardison quick-marched his men toward the bank. As they neared First National, Hardison observed a small group of men, miners to judge by their clothes, standing across the street and watching the bank.

Hardison called a halt and approached the four miners. When they saw his militia uniform, all four moved toward him.

"Cap'n." Nodded one man. "You come at a good time. Somethin' don't look right at that bank."

The militiaman shot a quick glance over at the bank—everything seemed quiet. He turned his gaze on the miner and waited for an explanation.

"We got here about five minutes ago," the man explained. "We seen three men ride up to the bank an' go in. One of 'em was carrying his Winchester. Ain't nobody come or gone since. It just don't look right. Who needs his Winchester in a bank?"

"Stay here," Hardison commanded. He sent three of his men to the alley on the far side of the bank and across the street. His orders were to fire only if fired upon. Hardison took the last man and stationed the two of them in the alley next to a hardware store and directly across from the bank.

"Stand ready to fire, but wait for my command," he ordered. They pressed themselves against the wall of the hardware store, rifles at the ready, and watched the bank. Glare from the early morning sun kept Hardison from seeing anything through the front window.

The door flew open suddenly, and three men spilled out onto the boardwalk in front of the bank. Hardison stepped away from the wall, lifting his Winchester. The militiaman next to him did the same. Hardison heard the echo of his own voice, commanding the robbers to halt.

The next events happened so quickly that Hardison later remembered them as all happening at once. The robber in front lifted a pistol he was carrying. Hardison's shot and the one coming from the man next to him sounded like one. The man they had targeted staggered back, dropping his pistol and a gunny sack.

Hardison was never sure if the other two robbers in front of the bank heard his command to drop their weapons. The one on the left, carrying a Winchester in front of him, lifted his rifle, while the other clawed a pistol out of his gun belt. All five militiamen fired, causing a deafening roar in the street.

As the echoing sounds died away, Hardison slowly lowered his Winchester and stared across the street. All three robbers were down, and he could see no sign of movement. He ordered his men to hold their positions.

Hardison slowly crossed the street, bringing his rifle back up into a firing position as he crossed. He wasn't worried about the men lying on the porch. He was worried that there might be one or two more inside the bank, waiting for him.

Reaching the boardwalk, Hardison stepped up but

stayed crouched as he kicked away the guns dropped by the robbers when they fell. He waved for his men to advance across the street and waited for them to reach him.

Hardison, still crouched, moved to stand beside the bank door and tapped it with his gun butt. "State militia!" he yelled. "I'm coming in!"

He yanked the door open and burst through, swinging his Winchester back and forth. A man at the back came to his knees and staggered forward, waving his hands in the air. "Bank president!" he called in a hoarse cry. "Don't shoot. They are all gone."

━━━

An examination of the bodies on the porch showed that one man matched a poster sent by Lat Smith. Hardison still didn't have a name for him, but the young guy with the prominent nose was the first one they had shot when he led the charge out of the bank.

Hardison dispatched a man to fetch the town doctor. He sent a second man to get a wagon and supervise the removal of the bodies. Stepping back inside, he asked the bank president and employees what they could tell him about the robbers.

As it turned out, the bank employees, though uninjured, weren't of much help. Nobody had recognized any of the robbers. One man had called another by the name of Clyde when he called a second man to join him in the vault. That turned out to be the only thing Hardison could learn from the bank staff.

Two militiamen helped the bank president carry

the stolen money back inside, where they locked it back into the vault. The president gave the other employees the rest of the day off and closed the bank for the day.

Standing on the porch as the bank president locked the door behind him, Hardison ordered two men to stay in front of the bank while he went to find the five men he had sent to guard the other three banks.

He was saved the search when he saw the Leadville sheriff, who had met them at the train station, moving toward them on horseback. The sheriff, named Potter, reined in and waved at Hardison.

"The other banks are open and safe," he called, eyeing the three corpses being loaded into the undertaker's wagon. "Looks like you've been busy." He turned his gaze back to Hardison. "I left your men on duty at the other banks," he said. "But your men arrested a guy after he set fire to a wagon full of hay outside the Silver Bow Bank. I have him in my jail. Thought you might wanna have a little talk with him."

"You thought right." Hardison trotted down the steps and mounted up. Maybe, he thought, he could finally find out who these guys were.

━━━

Hardison leaned against the cell bars, more than a little surprised when he saw the prisoner. This guy was young—just a kid, really. He was huge, but Hardison thought he looked a little scared.

Sheriff Potter leaned against the wall across from

the cell and behind Hardison. "He said his name was Ox," he told Hardison.

"Ox," Hardison repeated. "What name did your mama call you?"

The kid shrugged and said nothing.

"Your friends are all dead," Hardison told him. "They got themselves shot trying to rob a bank here."

The kid's head came up in surprise, but he stared at Hardison and said nothing.

Hardison reached into his pocket and pulled out the poster. He spread it open and held it up against the bars. "This one's dead," he said, pointing. "Two more after him. One of 'em had a sling on his shoulder. Looks like he'd been shot."

Ox's head came up again and he slumped against the wall of his cell. "Henry," he mumbled. "My mama named me Henry."

"You thirsty, Henry?" The kid nodded, so Hardison passed a canteen through the cell bars and began asking questions.

Half an hour later, Hardison figured he had learned everything this kid knew about the outlaw gang they'd been chasing. The man in the poster was Harvey Brown, and the other two robbers were brothers named Clyde and Jessie Rust. Ox, or Henry Miller, was the prisoner. All were from Trinidad.

Harvey, who said he was working for his uncles, had come to Trinidad and promised them some good money for doing a couple of holdups. Ox didn't know the names of Harvey's uncles, but Harvey had bragged about a robbery in Silverton a little while back.

Ox said that he and his friends had been behind the recent bank robbery in Pueblo.

Hardison had pressed Ox hard about where the rest of the gang was and what they planned on doing next. Ox insisted this was the last robbery he, Clyde, and Jessie had planned on doing. Harvey had told them the three of them should go home after this robbery, and maybe Harvey would have something else for them later.

Ox said he didn't know where Harvey's uncles were, what their names were, or anything else. He said Harvey had said something once about catching a train to Durango after this robbery, but that was all Ox knew. He laid down on his bunk in the cell with his back to the bars and said nothing else.

Hardison got directions to the telegraph office and trotted over to send the information to Lat Smith. Then he relieved his men of duty at the four banks and took them to the nearest café to celebrate with some steak and beer.

Warner had done one more thing on his way out of Durango after shooting the two men who had tried to stage a holdup. He wasn't worried too much about pursuit after shooting the two men. Anybody from shantytown who had come to look things over would have seen that each man had been shot through the heart. Folks got a lot less curious after seeing something like that.

No, Warner was thinking more about the holdup

the Castles planned to stage in Durango. He was still in favor of the holdup. There was some good money in that town, and the First National Bank of Durango was the only real bank in the town. Warner would stay with the Castle brothers for the holdup. He just wasn't sure how long he wanted their little partnership to last after the robbery.

For starters, that robbery in Pueblo, the one master-minded by the Castles' nephew, that robbery had been botched. Maybe worse, the newspaper said all the outlaws had gotten away. Warner knew the plan was for them to go up to Leadville afterward and hold up a bank there. What if one of 'em got caught up there?

Harvey, he was sure, knew enough about all of them to leave them all swinging at the end of a rope if he talked to the law. Not likely he would turn in his uncles, though. Blood was thicker than water. Everybody knew that. Harvey would serve up Warner on a silver platter to save his own neck.

Warner would give the newspaper he'd bought to the Castles and see what they had to say about the botched robbery. He would help with the robbery in Durango. After that, though, he needed to have his own plans, starting with how and when he left the Durango bank. He might go out with the Castles, or he might not.

Warner had scouted the back alley behind the bank. Just as he had expected, there was a back door. Lots of banks had a back door for deliveries, or to move a lot of money from the vault without people seeing all that money and getting ideas.

Outlaws like himself didn't much like the idea of

leaving by the back door. One lawman or just a town shopkeeper with a gun at both ends of the alley could bottle a man up with nowhere to go.

Still, if he let the Castles burst out that front door while he waited and slipped out the back...that might be something to think about. Now, on the way out of town, following the railroad track, he was turning over another idea in his head.

Warner followed the tracks for about a mile or two out of town, noting that the climb into the San Juan Mountains and a few sharp curves would force the train to slow down in a couple spots. He was guessing that the train would have to slow to fifteen miles an hour or less to take the turns.

Warner reined in his horse where the tracks began a steeper climb into the mountains and thought things over. There were ladders on the sides of most freight cars. A skilled horseman might just time things and jump from his horse to board a train. He'd heard of it being done. It was a pretty desperate move. After a little more thought, he resolved to think of a better way to board a train without being seen.

Satisfied he'd learned everything he needed to know before going back to the hideout, he moved out. He would be back to report to the Castles before dark this evening.

━━━

Now seated across the campfire on the mesa, Warner watched as Bryce Castle read the article in the Durango newspaper. A vein rose in the older Castle's forehead and began throbbing as he worked his way through the report. Warner remained silent as Bryce crumpled the newspaper and tossed it aside.

Warner dug into his pocket, pulled out a cigar from the general store in Durango, and lit it while Bryce got up to pace.

"Got another one?" The question caught him by surprise.

Warner stared across the fire at Tom Castle for a while, then reluctantly dug into his pocket and tossed one across the fire. When Bryce stopped and stared, Warner shook his head.

"Got no more," he lied. There were four more in his saddlebag, but he didn't feel like sharing. Bryce went back to pacing, then wheeled to look at Warner.

"You been in the bank? Know anything about it?"

"Nope." Warner shook his head. This was another lie. He'd been inside to check it out, and of course, he knew about the back door. It might come in handy later if he was the only one who knew about that before they got into the bank. He decided to toss a bone to Bryce.

"There's just the one bank," he said. "First National Bank of Durango."

Bryce mumbled something and went back to pacing. "We'll have to hit 'em right away," Bryce snapped.

Warner's head came up. He couldn't believe what he'd just heard with his own ears. Tom Castle's jaw dropped. They both stared across the campfire. Bryce Castle was the most cautious of them. Now, he wheeled around and glared at the other two.

"What? By now, those idiots are in Leadville, prob'ly gettin' ready to rob that bank. They might git themselves shot. They'll have badges out everywhere if that happens. We've got to move now!"

Warner shook his head and shifted uneasily. "What if they git captured? What if they tell the law about us?"

Bryce settled a glare on Warner. "Harvey won't talk. He knows better," Bryce snarled.

Warner didn't blink. "What about those boys he knows that he's bringin' in for the job? What about them?"

Bryce shot a glance over at his brother Tom, who shrugged and waited. Bryce stared at the ground, obviously considering this for the first time. "Harvey won't tell them nothin'," he decided. He stuck to his decision and barked his orders.

"We break camp an' mount up at first light! By tomorrow, we'll be sizin' things up in Durango." He glared at Warner again. "Tom and me will be lookin' things over in Durango. Warner, you'll stay out of town! Nobody gets another look at you in that town till we're riding out with their money."

▭

Warner dropped off the back car of the train in Durango and kept his head down while he waited for his horse to be unloaded. After that, he mounted up and rode directly out of town. Those were Bryce's orders, but he didn't so much care about that. He would settle in at that abandoned mine tunnel outside shantytown and wait there until he met the Castle brothers on the edge of shantytown on Thursday night. That was two nights from tonight, and he had nothing to do meanwhile. That was fine with Warner. This heist had started to feel dangerous. The Castle brothers could take the risks from here on in.

Moving out of town, Warner spotted a run-down general store near shantytown. He swung down, tethered his horse, and walked in. A guy with only one eye was ringing up sales. Warner picked up some beans and crackers, looking for whiskey. He didn't see any but stepped up to the counter at the back.

"Got any whiskey?" he asked as he thumped the beans and the cracker on the countertop.

The clerk looked him over, thought about it, then ducked and retrieved a bottle of whiskey from the shelf under the counter. Warner passed some money across the counter, got his change, and walked out.

Bryce Castle settled into a seat by the window across the street from First National Bank of Durango, ordered some food, and watched the people going into the bank. Some things he was already sure he knew about this bank. There were a lot of miners in the area, along with a smelter to process ore coming in from Silverton. That meant the bank would have a constant stream of customers on Saturday mornings. The smelter workers and miners would be there in force.

Castle was more interested right now in watching for activity from the merchants. Monday was more likely to be the big banking day for merchants, but this town had a big railroad presence and a lot of shops. Today was a Tuesday. He wanted to see how many merchants were banking today.

His brother Tom was watching the lawmen in town. There was a sheriff's office here, they knew that. Tom would watch the sheriff and look for any deputies the sheriff might have around town. They would also need to know if there was a Colorado militia presence. Bryce himself would also watch for guards at the bank.

The next few days should tell the tale on whether they could get out of this town, and maybe out of Colorado, with a big payday in their saddlebags.

FIFTEEN
WAITING AND WATCHING

Tom Castle looked around him at the diner where the brothers had gone for dinner. It was a sagging barn-like building attached to the railroad depot. He poked a spoon into the bowl of beef stew the waiter had just set in front of him. He growled under his breath and glared across the table at his brother.

"What's the matter with the saloons?" he muttered. "You can get yourself a good steak an' some beer at some of them saloons. This stew tastes like somebody just shot a raccoon out back."

"We don't want nobody to remember our faces around here," Bryce Castle hissed. "Too many people at the saloons, too much goin' on there. Eat yer raccoon stew and I'll git you some beer."

They had been in Durango for just a day. Tom Castle had some good news and some bad news for his brother. There was a sheriff and just one deputy who spent most of his time as a blacksmith. There was no militia in town that he could see. That was the good news. The bad news was he'd seen another badge around town, and he was pretty sure it was a marshal. He waited for the beer to arrive before he gave his brother the bad news.

Bryce stopped with his spoon halfway to his mouth. "Marshal?" he hissed. "What makes you think it was a marshal?"

Tom Castle shrugged and gulped down two massive swallows of his beer. "He had hisself a badge. When he come out of the sheriff's office, the sheriff called him Marshal."

Bryce let out a moan and slumped back in his chair. "What's his name? What's he doin' here?"

Tom finished his beer with another long gulp and looked around for the waiter. "Dunno," he said. "I follered 'em around for a while, but they just went down to the telegraph office and then walked around town for a bit. They didn't go to the bank."

Bryce cursed under his breath for a while and ordered himself another beer when Tom got a refill. He shoveled his stew down his throat while the waiter brought the second beer. When the bowl of stew and the beer glass were both empty, he announced his decision.

"You and me are gonna switch tomorrow. You watch the bank, and I'll follow this marshal guy around. You saw him at the sheriff's office and the telegraph office, right?"

Tom nodded. "Whaddya want me to watch for at the bank?"

Bryce stared out the window, wondering if the marshal was sending a telegram to get more tin stars in town. Or was there maybe news about Harvey and his boys robbing a bank in Leadville? Finally, he remembered his brother had asked him a question.

"Guards," he said finally. "Watch for guards. Let me know if the sheriff or this marshal guy start sniffing around at that bank."

I was about to wear a trail from my boardinghouse room to the telegraph office. I needed news from Captain Hardison on things in Leadville. If the outlaw gang wasn't operating up there, I needed Hardison and his men down here.

It was my third day in town, and finally, I had a message from Hardison waiting for me. When I read the message, I was glad I had left Hardison and his squad in Leadville. I sent a fast reply to Hardison, then I took the message down to *Ma's Bakery* and had a seat while Ma made a fuss over me. I was hoping Sheriff Carnes would show up, and he did, just about the time I was tucking into some bacon, eggs, and fresh-baked bread. Ma disappeared into the kitchen and got busy again with some breakfast for Carnes.

Carnes plopped into a chair and eyed my breakfast. I shoved the telegram from Hardison across the table to give him something else to look at. I didn't need him drooling over my breakfast.

Carnes read the telegram and let out a low whistle. Hardison reported he had stopped a robbery and killed three men, including the kid in the poster. His name, as the telegram told me, was Harvey Brown. Two other outlaws I hadn't heard of had been killed, and Hardison had taken a fourth man prisoner.

Carnes read it again and grinned. "I bet the guvnor's happy," he observed.

I reached for my coffee and grunted. "Happy for now, I guess," I said, "but if they pull off another robbery here, it won't last long. I told Hardison and his men to hightail it down here. His telegram said he expects to catch a train arriving at eight o'clock on Saturday morning."

Carnes's grin faded, then perked up when his breakfast arrived. He took a few bites while he thought about what I had just said. "Whaddya want to do?" he asked. "That's a lot of firepower that ain't here yet. We've got a couple days between then and now to hold 'em off."

I nodded unhappily and stared out the window, wondering if the guy with the scar and some other robbers were gettin' ready to go after Durango's bank. I knew it was a rich target.

"You've just got one deputy, right?" I asked.

Carnes nodded. "Yup. And he's part-time. Most of the time, he's the blacksmith in this town."

I leaned my elbows on the table. "I've been tryin' to decide," I told him. "Do I want to show myself at that bank where they can see me—if they're watching the place, that is—or do I want them to think they could walk right in and take the money? Then catch 'em on the way out."

"Hmmph." Carnes thought that one over for a long

time. "I don't guess we've got enough badges and manpower to scare 'em off. Maybe we want 'em to think they could walk right in and knock the place over. We could take those boys down on the way out, like you said. Get the drop on 'em."

"That's the way I'm leanin'," I said. "At least until Hardison gets here with the militia. You can't hide that many guys, anyway, so we'll post them around the bank when they get here. By that time, maybe we'll have a lead on these robbers, and we could take the fight to them."

I leaned back and thought it over a little more. "Your deputy, the blacksmith," I said. "What's his name?"

Carnes answered around a mouthful of eggs. "Saylor. Bart Saylor."

"Could he spare us a few hours to look things over? Without his badge, I mean. He could go into the bank for some blacksmith business and look things over. He probably does business there, I'm guessing. If there's outlaws hanging around and watching the bank, where might they be? Saloon, café?"

"Café. There's a café right across the street. I'd say that's likely."

Just then, a miner, or somebody dressed like a miner, came into the café. His eyes fell on my badge as he walked past, and he seemed to give me a long look. I watched as he went to the counter and bought a pie. I'd been around a lot of miners in my time, and those weren't miner's hands on that guy. Those miner boys had calluses and, like as not, some bruises. This guy, when he reached out to pay, had hands like a librarian or a schoolmarm.

I tried to memorize his face when he walked out. After a minute, I realized Carnes had asked a question.

"Sorry," I said, "did you notice that guy who just walked past? Do you know him?"

Carnes shook his head. "Got a quick look at him. Don't think I've ever seen him. Why?"

I shook my head. "Somethin' funny about him, that's all. Prob'ly nothing." I tried to remember his question. It was about the blacksmith. "If he's got a couple hours he could give us," I said, "maybe he could look in at the bank and then have himself a meal in that café and see if anybody in there seems real interested in the bank."

Another thought crossed my mind. "Do you think I could talk to the bank president? Not at the bank, I mean. Maybe he could drop in at your office for a while?"

We stopped at the blacksmith's place. He was downright agreeable to going for a free breakfast, since I was paying. He agreed to stop at the sheriff's office later and tell me what he had seen at the bank and at the café.

I stopped at the telegraph office while Carnes went down to the bank to ask the president to come to the sheriff's office. Hardison had answered my last message. They would take the next train from Leadville, but that didn't leave until tomorrow. This was Thursday, so they would arrive in Durango by eight o'clock Saturday morning. That gave me just two days to hold down the lid on this place until then.

I moved on down to Sheriff Carnes's office and waited. The bank president was a little huffy when he first showed up, not happy I had pulled him away from his work. He settled down some when I told him I was tryin' to prevent a robbery at his bank.

I started asking about the weekly routines there. He told me the bank usually had the most money in it by about noon on Mondays. The miners and the workers at the smelter brought their money in on Saturdays, but they kept a fair amount on 'em for the saloons and gambling halls on Saturday night. The shopkeepers brought money at different times, but a lot of them came on Monday mornings. He wasn't expecting any big payrolls anytime soon.

"Do I need guards? I could get some in here by next week sometime." He looked at me, then over at Carnes.

I shook my head. "By then, I'm gonna have all the manpower I need," I told him. "We'll keep an eye on things between now and then." I pointed at myself and Carnes.

━━━

Saylor, the blacksmith, came by about an hour later and reported in. "One guy," he said, "sat at a table by the window and spent a lot of time lookin' over toward the bank. Kept gettin' a refill on his coffee and lookin' over there. He finally paid up and left. Nuthin' special about him. He dressed like a drifter but wore a gun. I follered him over to the Statler Hotel."

My eyebrows went up a little. I didn't know what to think of that. The Statler was too pricey for me, and for sure too pricey for a drifter. My gut told me there were at least a couple guys in town that were up to no good, and this might be one of 'em. I hoped Hardison would be here in time to give me the upper hand if they tried anything. If they would just hold off for two days.

———

They met on the edge of shantytown, and Warner led them along a narrow trail beside the rails. Two miles later, the Castle brothers left the narrow trail and followed Warner up an embankment and into the yawning mouth of a cave. Leaving their horses at the entrance, Bryce and Tom Castle waited while Warner stepped inside and lit a lamp.

As they walked forward and let their eyes adjust to the dim light, they could see a few rocks arranged in a circle around the lamp. Bryce's eyes swept the cave. He could see some food and ammunition stacked against one wall. The remains of a small fire were near the entrance.

"How'd you find this place?"

Warner shrugged. "I've been scoutin' around out here while you boys were watching the town."

Bryce's eyes went back to the food and ammo. "Where'd you git that?" He pointed.

Warner shrugged. "Bought it off a couple guys

over there in shantytown. They was headed out of town."

Bryce knew when he was being lied to, but he let it pass. There were a few shabby stores he'd seen on the edge of town where they probably didn't care who you were as long as you had cash money to pay for things. Warner had probably gone to one of those stores.

Bryce leaned forward and got right to it. "We hit the bank Saturday morning," he said flatly. "Right after the miners and boys from the smelter put their week's pay in there."

Warner shot a glance at Tom Castle, who looked just as surprised as Warner felt. Bryce hadn't even shared his plans with his brother, clearly. His eyes went back to Bryce, who shot him a challenging look.

Warner's mind raced as he leaned back and waited to see if Tom Castle would say anything. Would there be enough money in a Saturday morning score for him to get away and have enough money to go to California or Texas? The net would close in on him here sooner or later if he stayed.

Tom said nothing. He stared at Warner, waiting.

"We ain't never moved that fast," Warner objected. "We only bin in town two days."

Bryce was ready for that one. "Only law in town right now besides the sheriff is a marshal. He looks kinda salty, but there's only one of him. The sheriff don't look like much. That marshal, though, he checks the telegraph office so often I think he's expectin' reinforcements around here. Mebbe he's heard something. Mebbe Harvey and his boys hit the bank in Leadville already and we just ain't heard about it yet. We've got to move before this marshal gits hisself some help."

Warner shook his head. "Saturday ain't even a weekday. That's when the shopkeepers bring money, on weekdays. You expectin' a big payroll or somethin' to hit that bank on Friday?"

"Nope. There's money in there, though," Bryce snapped back. "There ain't but the one bank in town, and they've got the railroad, the shops, the miners, the ore smelting—all of 'em puttin' money in that bank."

Warner had another objection. "We ain't got anybody to set a fire or an explosion or nuthin' to throw everybody off the scent, like we always done before. What about that?"

Bryce shrugged. "We don't have nobody, like you said. If Harvey shows up, he can do it. Right now, we've just got us. All of us gotta be at that bank."

Bryce stood and started pacing. Warner knew the signs. Bryce had a nasty temper, and Warner had pushed things far enough. He leaned back and nodded. "How we gonna do this? And what time? I'll have to meet you boys at the bank, I guess."

Bryce left off pacing and sat down. "Yep. You meet us there at ten o'clock sharp. The miners and boys from the smelting plant will have left their money in there by then." He pointed at Warner. "You and me will take the vault and the cages. Tom will watch the customers, the tellers, and the front door. In and out, just like that. You'll see."

"Ten o'clock," Warner agreed. He said nothing else while the Castle brothers walked back to the mouth of the cave, mounted their horses, and left.

Warner had a feeling Bryce Castle planned to leave the front door of that bank first, along with his brother. He would let Warner leave last and take any fire coming from the street.

Warner moved to the campfire site at the mouth of the cave and built a small fire. He warmed his hands for a while, then got up and opened a can of beans to heat over the fire. He didn't plan to leave by the front door. He would go out the back. That could either happen peacefully or not. He could take down Bryce Castle if he needed to.

The train out of Leadville was an hour late leaving the station. Hardison was frustrated, but there was nothing he could do. More coal had to be loaded into the tender car, or they might simply stop en route when they ran out of steam. Hardison sent two of his troopers to help with the shoveling.

Now, finally, they were well underway. Hardison knew that Lat Smith was probably counting on him to be there for Saturday's business at the bank. Monday might be more critical, but he knew every day mattered.

Hardison tried to relax on the narrow wooden seat. The train seemed to cling impossibly to the shoulders of the mountain. The slope beside them tumbled away into a forest of pine and fir. Hardison leaned back and tried to doze.

His nap was shaken by the grinding, screeching noise of the engine's brakes. Hardison was thrown into the seat in front of him. Passengers around him cried out in both pain and fear as the train ground to a halt.

The conductor hustled past him on his way to the engine. Hardison instinctively jumped up and followed him. The conductor, glancing back, saw him but offered no objection. A few minutes later, standing in the engine, Hardison could see the problem. A rock-slide had completely blocked the tracks!

The engineer and conductor conferred in low tones. Moments later, Hardison understood what had to be done. The rocks would have to be manually lifted and cleared. Hardison immediately volunteered his men and volunteered to find other men on the train who would help.

Soon after, a crew of twenty men set to work on the rock pile. Sweating despite the cold air, they piled their jackets to the side and worked to clear the tracks, mindful of the dangerous position they were in. A misstep could send someone plunging over the edge.

Four hours later, exhausted and filthy, the crew cheered as the last rock went over the edge. The men trooped back into the train and waited as the train's crew shoveled coal, and the steam pressure built. Finally, with a blast and a cloud of steam, the engine moved out and continued the journey. Passengers and crew cheered as the train wound through the mountains again.

Hardison pulled the timepiece from his pocket and checked it. Together with the late start, the train was now running over five hours late. They would arrive in Durango after one o'clock on Saturday afternoon.

Hardison slumped against the back of his seat and reminded himself that there was nothing he could do. If he could send a telegram to Lat Smith at the next stop, he would. He would have his men ready for action when they arrived at Durango. He hoped they would get there soon enough to help.

SIXTEEN

TRAIN TROUBLES

I was at the Durango train station at seven thirty Saturday morning, ready for Hardison and his boys to give me a little more firepower in this town. I was sitting on a bench outside the station when the station agent came out the door, walking kinda slow like he had some bad news. I braced myself. I was right about the bad news.

"Train from Leadville has been delayed," he said. He got the bad news out in a hurry, I'll give him that. He sat down on the bench next to me.

"Rockslide closed down the tracks for a few hours," he explained. "They had to get out and clear the tracks themselves before they could get goin' again." He stopped for just a second to let that sink in. "I expect they'll be here around two or three this afternoon."

I looked at the clock by the station door and thought that one over. The bank would be open in a little over an hour. Hardison would be here too late to help today. I stood and looked at the station agent. "I've got eleven militiamen coming in on that train," I told him. "Tell Captain Hardison I said to get over to the bank with his men as soon as they can get here."

———

Sheriff Carnes looked up from his desk when I walked into the jail. "Howdy," he said. "Did your boys get into town?"

I shook my head and looked around the corner to check the cells. Carnes had two guys in jail this morning. Somebody was gonna have to keep an eye on them, I thought sourly. I slumped into a chair across from his desk.

"Rockslide," I mumbled. "My boys won't git here till two or three this afternoon."

Carnes turned his head toward the jail cells. "I can't just let these boys go," he said. "They ain't just a couple of Friday night drunks. There was a shootin' at one of the saloons last night." He thought for a minute. "I'll get my deputy, Saylor, to come down here and watch this place. I'll go to the bank with you."

Carnes went down to get his deputy, and I watched the jail while he did. Fifteen minutes later, Saylor had settled down in Carnes's office with a cup of coffee and a shotgun, and Carnes took the walk down to the bank with me. It would be another half hour before it opened.

"Your call," Carnes said. "Watch it from the inside or the outside?"

"Outside," I told him. "It can get a little rough

inside when they know you're in there with 'em. I don't want a teller or a customer to catch a stray bullet the robbers were aimin' at me." I turned around and looked at the café across the street. "Let's wait in there and watch for a while."

We took a seat by a window and watched while the bank opened, and a steady stream of customers came through. By their looks, most were miners. Some might have worked at the smelter, but a lot of those smelter workers were ex-miners, anyway. After an hour or two, the stream of customers thinned out, and I started to feel better about things. Like most banks I had seen, this one would close at noon, today being a Saturday.

They had all dressed up like miners for the holdup. Warner had to admit that it was smart, but the flannel shirt itched, the hobnailed boots hurt his feet, and the broad-brimmed hat made him feel like a preacher. He swore to himself as he walked along to the livery stable. These hobnailed boots would be the first thing to go. He was about to buy a horse he would only own for one day, if things went according to plan. On top of that, he would have to leave his own horse behind, and that was the best horse he had stolen in a long time.

A sharp-eyed old man watched him as he entered the livery stable and looked at the horses marked for sale. Warner stopped at a mustang crossbreed of some kind, maybe ten years old. He reached out to check the bay's teeth, then changed his mind when the horse laid his ears back.

"He'll go all day," the old man said in his ear. Warner jumped. He hadn't seen the old codger sneaking up on him.

"Yeah? How fast will he git me there? Looks kinda old to me. Is he gonna try to bite me all day, too?"

The old man backed off a step, showing some yellow teeth in a cagey smile. "You need a racehorse, that's gonna cost you a whole lot more than this horse. If you gotta leave town in a hurry, that'll cost you."

Warner cursed under his breath again and circled the bay mustang, checking his hooves. He noticed the old man had totally ignored the part about getting bit. "How much for this one?"

The old man shot a quick glance at Warner's miner clothes, wondering if this guy knew anything about horses. "One hunnerd."

Warner snorted and walked away. The old man tried again. "Ninety." Warner had almost reached the gate. "Seventy-five!"

Warner came back and took another look at the mustang. He pointed at a pile of old gear in the corner. "Gimme a saddle, bridle, bit, and reins. I'll give you ninety altogether."

The old man rocked back on his heels and took a bite of tobacco. His gut told him he wouldn't get any more for this horse. This man dressed like a miner, but he wore a pistol like he knew what to do with it. The old man nodded.

Warner handed over the ninety dollars, then picked out the gear he needed from the corner. He saddled the horse and led it out of the livery stable. The old man watched from the livery stable as Warner led the horse away. Warner moved over to a side street and followed the side street to a spot just behind the bank. Once there, he tethered the bay to the rail.

There were just two more stops to make before he met up with the other outlaws. Warner crossed the street, turned a corner, and walked into the train station. He ignored the station agent, pulled his hat down over his forehead, and studied the schedule for trains going to Silverton. A faint smile crossed his lips when he saw there was a train leaving at two o'clock this afternoon. He turned and left the train station, ignoring the station agent's questions.

Finally, he made a stop at the hardware store. Warner had ridden trains many times and had knowledge of hopping trains that would have surprised even the Castles. He had a feeling that was about to come in handy.

He looked around in the general store until he found a twenty-foot length of very stout rope. The owner wanted to chat while he rang up the sale, but Warner said nothing as he paid and left.

Warner looked around as he left the hardware store, but saw nobody watching him. He walked the six blocks to the café where he had left his horse, then went inside to join the Castle brothers. He turned up his collar to hide the scar on his cheek as he stepped inside.

"We go in right before it closes," Bryce Castle announced. "Bank closes at twelve noon, so we go in about ten minutes before that. Tom watches the door and gets customers and tellers on the ground. Warner empties the cages. I get the manager to open the vault and take what's in there. Warner can help if there's enough cash in the vault."

Warner nodded his head slightly. "What about locked drawers and such in the vault?" he asked. "Sometimes folks rent space in the vault. I've got an iron bar. I could force some of them open. Might be gold dust and such in there."

Bryce Castle stared at Warner for a second, then grunted. "Might be some cash or gold dust," he agreed. "Might just be a bunch of mining certificates and paper and such, though. We don't care about that." After another second, he nodded. "Okay, if there's time, you can do that. We leave when I say, no later."

Bryce threw a challenging look at Warner, who nodded. "When you say."

"Tom and me first," Bryce ordered. "Warner, you cover us and come last."

Warner nodded. That's the way he wanted it. This could save him a lot of trouble. He planned to leave last, no matter what he had to do to make that happen.

All three ordered some breakfast and waited until it was time to ride to the bank.

My mind had turned to Monday morning already. Hardison and his crew would be here by then. We could guard the bank and look around town a little at the same time. Checking a few saloons and cafés might turn up a few suspicious faces we would want to keep an eye on. Maybe we could catch anybody planning a robbery ahead of time.

I was checking my pockets for some money to leave on the table when three more customers showed up at the bank. There were two inside, making five customers in there. Carnes and I were going to go over to the bank now and stay while they closed and locked up.

"Miners," Carnes said, watching while the three of them tied up their horses and stepped inside.

"Looks like," I agreed, dropping some money on the table. "Let's wait across the street while these three and the two inside do their business, then we can go in and help 'em lock up."

The station agent came bustling in just then and left me a telegram just sent by Captain Hardison. He explained the rockslide, which, of course, I already knew about. He expected to be in town with his troops by three o'clock this afternoon. That would give them time to get a little rest before the bank opened for their busy day on Monday.

Carnes stopped to talk to a town merchant while I stepped outside, watching the bank. Something was wrong...the horses! All five horses were still tethered to the railing in front of the bank. It didn't make sense that nobody would have finished their business in the last ten minutes and stepped outside.

I held my hand in the air when I heard Carnes step outside behind me. "Get behind that pillar," I muttered, angling my head toward a pillar at the edge of the boardwalk. I stepped behind another one and pulled my Colt.

"It don't make sense nobody's come out of the bank yet," I said. "Get ready. If they bust outta there with their guns up, shoot first and ask questions later."

Warner's eyes swept the bank as they stepped inside. Only two tellers were working this morning, and the owner, or bank president, or whoever he was, was parked behind a desk near the vault at the back.

All three of the robbers wore a bandana over their mouths. They drew their guns as soon as they stepped inside. Two customers, probably smelter workers, were stuffing some money into their pants pockets. Warner gave them each a shove toward the back of the bank.

"Hey!" was the only word one of them managed after being shoved. Warner reversed his grip and slugged the man over the head with the butt of his gun. The customer collapsed to the floor. The other man laid down quietly and put his hands over his head. Both tellers opened their cash drawers and stepped back.

Warner produced a gunny sack and emptied the contents of the cash drawers into the sack within a few seconds. Stepping out from behind the cages, he heard the bank president arguing with Bryce Castle about opening the vault.

"Can't do it," he spluttered. "Folks trusted me with their money!" He eyed Castle's Colt. "You just do what you gotta do."

Warner stepped over to the man's desk and eyed a photograph propped up on the desk. He picked it up. Five people were posed stiffly on the front porch of a wooden house. A man and a woman stood in the back row, with three children in the front.

"Lookee here," Warner said, pointing at the man in the picture. "This here must be your family. Ain't that nice?" He pulled the picture in for a closer look. "And this must be your house. I'll bet I can find that house with no trouble." He locked eyes with the bank president. "Ain't that a shame about the kids? I mean, about their daddy bein' too stupid to open the vault."

The president swallowed hard, staggered to his feet, and stumbled over to the vault. Fifteen seconds later, it was open.

The shelves in the vault had stacks of paper money, along with some bags of gold dust and a lot of coins. Warner followed behind Castle, letting Castle stuff most of the paper money in his bag.

Warner pulled an iron rod from his belt and began prying open some of the drawers and boxes lining the walls. The first two drawers he opened were full of cash and gold coins.

"Anything?" Castle stared from across the vault and waited impatiently.

"Naw, just shares of stock and stuff," Warner lied. He pried open two more, waved his hands in the air in fake disappointment, then moved to help Castle finish bagging the cash, dust, and coins on the shelves.

"Go!" Castle barked. Warner followed him out of the vault. The tellers, smelter workers, and the bank president were all still lying on the floor.

"Clear?" Bryce yelled at his brother.

"Yup." Tom Castle pointed out the window. "Couple guys just come outta the café. They ain't doin' nuthin', just standin' there."

All three robbers moved to the front of the bank, guns out and ready. Bryce Castle led the way.

"Go!" He shoved the door open and burst through onto the boardwalk, gun level. Tom Castle followed behind. Warner stood poised and ready, gun up, but he never moved toward the front door.

Gunfire filled the air outside as soon as the Castle brothers reached the boardwalk. Warner was already turned and moving toward the back of the bank when the first shots broke out. His brain told him he'd heard at least five shots out there by now. He broke into a trot, going back to the vault.

The bank president had come up to his knees when he heard the gunfire. His eyes bulged as he stared at Warner.

Warner didn't bother reversing his grip this time. He laid the barrel of his Colt alongside the man's head and knocked him cold. Warner stopped in the vault just long enough to empty three more drawers full of cash and gold coins, then he was out the back door.

By the time he'd reached the side street, he had pulled his bandana down around his neck. He saw no one in the street. He wasted no time in tying the gunny sack onto the saddle horn. In seconds, he was aboard the livery stable mustang, trotting down the side street, heading out of town. He noticed the shooting had stopped, back there at the bank.

I had one eye on the bank door and the other on those horses tied up out front. If I was counting this right, there were three robbers in there, and only two of us out here. I didn't like those odds. I shot a glance over at Carnes. He looked ready.

The bank door burst open and a guy wearing a bandana came flying out the door, gun up, with a gunny sack in his hand. That was enough for me. "Hold it!" I shouted.

He wheeled, gun up, looking for who had yelled at him. My gun came level just as he spotted me and fired. We exchanged shots. His bullet buried itself in the pillar next to me. Mine hit him square in the chest and he staggered back. He came up against the bank wall, gun still up, trying to get another shot at me. My second shot hit him square in the chest again. He dropped the gun and slid slowly down the wall.

I swung around to see how Carnes was doing. He was down on one knee, holding his right shoulder with his left hand and exchanging gunfire with the second robber, who had untied his horse and was trying to swing aboard.

My first shot at this second man knocked the robber down into the street. When he tried to get to his knees, my second shot put him down for good.

"You okay?" I yelled at Carnes. He came slowly to his feet and ducked behind the cover of the pillar. He nodded slowly. "I ain't hurt bad," he growled, "but I ain't shootin' too straight, neither."

"Stay there," I barked. I turned to study the two men who had come through that door. Both were down and not moving. I knew where those shots had gone, so I wasn't really worried about these two. I was worried about the owner of that other horse. Where was that guy?

It was deadly quiet inside that bank, and I couldn't just stay here. There could be several people at risk inside. I came up to a crouch and dashed across the street, moving just enough from side to side to present a difficult target.

I stopped over the guy in the street just long enough to kick his gun away. I did the same for the guy on the porch. I would leave it for a doc to decide if they were really dead. What I knew was that they didn't have enough breath to come after me right now.

I crouched beside the front door to the bank. Should I announce myself and go in, or might that just make me target number one for robber number three? If there was a teller or customer in there with a gun, they might be a little trigger-happy right at this minute. I couldn't blame them if they were.

Finally, I decided on a little of both. I yelled, "Marshal," as I yanked that door open and came bursting through. Nobody fired at me. I heaved a deep sigh and swung my Colt from side to side.

"Where's the other one?" I yelled. I got a bunch of blank looks as tellers and two guys dressed like miners came up off the floor. "Where's the other robber? There's another horse out there!"

I heard Carnes call out behind me, and I stood aside to let him in. "Keep an eye on things out here," I told him. "I've got to check the vault."

A quick look in the vault told me it had been cleaned out pretty good, and the third robber wasn't in there, either. I came out and squatted down next to the bank president. We had talked at the sheriff's office just yesterday, but his eyes weren't focused. I don't think he recognized me. I helped him into the chair behind his desk. There was a knot on his head the size of an egg.

"How many robbers?" I asked.

He rubbed the side of his head, moaned, and thought it over. "Three," he said. "One out front and two in the vault."

"Only two came out the front," I said.

He got to his feet slowly and looked around the corner. "I think maybe the other one went out the back," he mumbled. "He sledged me a good one with his pistol on the way out. He was headed for the back."

I whirled around, found a back door to the place, and went out, gun first. There was only an empty alley. I walked slowly along the alley until I came to a side street. There was nobody in sight, but I knew he had to have gone this way. Somebody had ridden away with at least a third of the bank's money.

I was still talking to the people at the bank for a long time after they hauled away the two dead bank robbers. Sheriff Carnes brought his posters over, but these guys didn't match anybody in the posters. Neither one of them was the guy with the face scar on the poster I had sent out before. The third robber who got away could have been the guy with the scar, but all of them wore bandanas covering their faces, so there was no way to tell.

I started by talking with the bank president. He told me how he'd refused to open the vault until one of them threatened his family. We went into the vault, and he showed me where some kind of pry tool had been used to open locked drawers. He couldn't estimate how much money had been taken, but he said these were wealthy miners and merchants who had rented these drawers.

The last thing he told me was that it was the third man, the escaped robber, who had hit him with a revolver and likely had left out the back. He saw enough of the man's beard to say he was dark-haired and probably over six feet tall. "Cold eyes," was the only other description he could give me.

One of the other two customers who had been in the bank was another man who'd been hit over the head with a pistol. From his description, it sounded like the same man who had hit the president had knocked this guy out.

The tellers weren't really able to add anything for me. I let everybody leave to go home, and I was now at the hitching rack out front, going through the saddlebag on the horse that had been left unclaimed after the robbery.

The saddlebag was completely empty, which made me think the third robber had planned to escape out the back the entire time, leaving this horse out front. I made a note of the brand on the horse, but I was willing to bet it had been stolen.

It was about then that Captain Hardison showed up with his ten men. The station agent brought them directly over from the train. I told Hardison's men to get themselves some food at the café across the street and sent Carnes to have a doctor look at his shoulder. I asked Hardison to sit with me while I caught him up on things.

Hardison sat down with me on a bench outside the bank while I talked about how to look for this third guy. It was no use trying to track him out of town. There were far too many tracks, and we had no way to know which route he had used to get out.

I took a pad of paper and a pencil out of my pocket

and started listing the most likely ways this guy could have left town. At the top of my list was the railroad to Silverton. If a guy wanted to lie low and let the heat simmer down, Silverton was a perfect little town.

The second most likely route I put down was the train south to Alamosa. From there, you could work your way over to Santa Fe and then to California. California seemed like a good place to spend all that stolen money.

The only other route I listed was by horse or wagon south into New Mexico. He could lose himself down there in New Mexico pretty fast if he wanted to. Still, it seemed to me this guy would likely want to get away faster than he could do it on horseback.

Hardison mostly listened and waited for orders. "All of it makes sense to me," he said. "How can my men help?"

I stood and tucked the paper and pencil back into my pocket. "While your boys are eating," I said, "let's go over to the train station and see if anybody remembers anything over there. I doubt he hopped a train here, but we can ask."

We drew a blank at the train station. I was afraid we would. Either this guy was smart enough to disguise himself when he got on, or he would board at a smaller station down the line.

I looked over at Hardison. "Get yourself something to eat," I said, "then send me two of your boys and I'll check the rail line north to Silverton for a while. Take three boys yourself and check the line to the south. Take a couple days on that. Have the rest of 'em ask questions around town."

Hardison saluted and started to move away, then I thought of something else and stopped him. "He left his horse in front of the bank," I said, "and I can't believe he walked out of town. Send a couple of your boys to the livery stable and see what they can turn up over there. Have the boys in town ask around about stolen horses."

━━

I was packing up for a little ride along the rails to the north when two of Hardison's boys showed up. They'd found something, I could see that from the looks on their faces.

"At the livery stable, sir," one of them said. "A man with real cold eyes and a nasty scar on his face bought a mustang over there just this morning. Paid for a saddle and some gear, along with the horse. Paid ninety dollars. The old man at the livery doesn't know the guy's name or where he went. The old man said he would have been scared to try checking up on this guy."

Finally! I had tied Scarface in with this gang of robbers. I wondered if there were any other outlaws left alive after Leadville and today's shootings. I didn't know where Scarface might have gone, but I'd already laid out the search for Hardison's boys and for me to start looking. That was more than what I'd had this morning.

I met up with the two men Hardison assigned to me out in front of the bank. We started at the train station and followed the rails north. I planned to check all the ground between here and the stop at Rock-wood. The train would have to stop there to take on water and fuel. After that, it would be some mighty tough country to ride through.

He'd had to camp overnight when dusk closed in, but he had been up and moving at daylight, and now had arrived at the place where he could finish making his escape.

Warner stripped the saddle and bridle from the mustang before turning him loose. Maybe the horse would find a herd of wild mustangs and live, maybe he wouldn't. Warner didn't really care about that. He just couldn't be bothered with this horse anymore.

He had stopped near the railroad stop at Rock-wood. No passengers would board here. There was just a tank with some water and a wooden shack to store fuel. He could see a cart already loaded with coal, waiting for the train to arrive. Warner settled into some brush about one hundred yards from the station and waited. The train wasn't going to get here for another hour, according to the schedule.

While he waited, Warner opened the gunny sack he had hauled with him from the bank. Getting aboard the train with this sack made things a lot tougher, but of course he wasn't going to leave it behind.

There were a few small bags of gold dust. He hefted them in his hand to estimate the weight, then set them aside. Next, he counted the gold coins, then the cash. Warner was guessing he had about five hundred dollars from this morning's robbery. Nice haul for a morning's work, and he wouldn't be sharing it with the Castle brothers. From the gunfire he'd heard there in town, that partnership was dissolved.

Knowing the train's arrival would wake him, Warner re-tied the gunny sack and settled himself down for a nap. Forty-five minutes later, he could hear the train whistle and feel the tracks rumbling as the train rolled into the station.

Keeping low, Warner scrambled from his hideout and ran to duck behind a stack of firewood near the siding. He watched as the crew hustled to swing out the waterspout to refill the water and offload coal into the tender just in front of the water tank.

Now came the trickiest part. He had to make the dash from his hiding spot behind the firewood to a gondola car—an open-sided car. There were several on this train. A few were empty, but that wouldn't work. He needed to be able to conceal himself, at least until the train was underway again.

Warner grabbed his saddlebag and the gunny sack and watched the crew working with the water and coal. He also kept a wary eye open for the train's engineer and conductor.

He picked out the second gondola car in the line as his target. It appeared to be carrying some scrap metal, hopefully enough to give him cover. With one last check on the crew, Warner dashed across the open ground, tossing saddlebag and gunny sack onto the car before pulling himself aboard and rolling to a stop behind a large chunk of metal.

He waited for shouts and approaching footsteps. He eased his right hand down and pulled his Colt from the holster. After a few minutes, he relaxed. Nobody had seen him boarding the train. After another fifteen minutes, he heard the loud sound of steam escaping the engine, and they slowly rolled away from the station.

Warner waited only until the train rounded a bend and the Rockwood station disappeared from view before he started moving again. It was only five miles to the next stop, and he could be spotted too easily if the train stopped to pick up a crew member or a passenger there.

Holding his bags, Warner walked steadily to the front of the gondola car. The next car in line was a boxcar—another reason he had chosen this gondola car to board. He needed to get into the cover of that boxcar. He had seen that the sliding door at the side of the boxcar was open just enough.

Warner only glanced down once at the coupling between the cars as he scooted along the coupling and onto the back of the boxcar. He looked up, knowing this part would be difficult and dangerous. He slung his saddle over his shoulder, then tied the gunny sack around his wrist.

Next, he climbed slowly and carefully up the ladder at the back of the boxcar. He reached the roof after a scary thirty seconds of climbing, hanging on to the ladder when the train swayed around corners.

Warner laid on the rooftop for a few minutes, catching his breath and letting the sweat roll down his cheeks and onto the rooftop. He could feel the train climbing into the mountains. He had to move now. The climb on the upward grade would slow the train enough to give him a chance.

Crawling toward the edge of the roof, Warner pulled the twenty-foot rope from his saddlebag and tied it securely to a beam running along the top of the boxcar, near the edge. He then threw the saddlebag over the side. He had no further use for it.

When he reached the edge of the roof, gunny sack still tied around his wrist, he stared down and adjusted his position to be perfectly above the opening in the side of the car. Warner took a few running steps and leaped off the edge of the roof. His momentum carried him out, then he came swinging back at the boxcar, holding onto the rope.

He made it through narrowly. His left shoulder took a painful hit on the edge of the open door, but his momentum was enough to carry him into the car. He landed on the balls of his feet, then tumbled sideways. He rolled up against a bag of grain and came to a stop.

Warner stood and checked himself over. Other than a throbbing shoulder, he was intact, and more importantly, the gunny sack was still attached to his wrist. He untied it now and stowed it behind several sacks of grain. A quick check told him the rawhide thong over the hammer had done its job and the Colt was still in his holster.

His heart was still pounding from the danger of what he'd just done. Warner paced back and forth in the boxcar, looking idly at the cargo until he felt calmer. When the train made its stop at Tacoma, he ducked behind the grain sacks, Colt at the ready.

Sometimes the conductor or brakeman came through the boxcars, checking the cargo.

The train pulled away from the Tacoma station, and as Warner relaxed, he found himself growing sleepy. He laid down behind the grain sacks, using one as a pillow. He tucked his pistol under his arm and slowly drifted off to sleep. He didn't awaken until he felt his ribs being prodded by the toe of someone's boot.

━━

We worked the ground along the rail line running north out of Durango, looking for tracks left behind by that third robber—the one with the scarred face. Hardison had sent me his best tracker, a guy from Tennessee named Hobbes.

The rail line ran along the steep hillsides covered with fir trees and pine, then dropped into steep canyons. We searched the ground to each side of that rail line, but there wasn't much hope of finding tracks unless they were fresh.

I had Hobbes concentrate on the wet ground where mountain streams cut across the trail, or along the banks of the Animas River, which the rail line followed through the mountains.

We had left Durango with just a few hours of daylight left. It was near sundown in the fading dusk light that Hobbes let out a cry as he kneeled near the bank of a rushing mountain stream. He waved a hand in the air at me.

"Here!" he called as I approached. He pointed at something on the ground.

Sure enough, when I rode up and dismounted, I found him pointing at a set of tracks. Somebody had crossed this stream on horseback, and pretty recently, from what I could tell.

"How long ago, do you think?" I asked Hobbes.

His forehead wrinkled up as he leaned in for a closer look. "Not long," he said finally, "mebbe this afternoon sometime."

My hopes rose. I stood and looked at the overhead sun, then called in my other militiaman. "We camp here," I announced. "I think our guy is headin' north, looking for a place to board the train. We'll pick up his trail again in the morning."

━━

Picking it up in the morning turned out to be a lot tougher than I thought, and I'd already thought it was going to be mighty hard. We fanned out and started the search right after sunrise, with a little coffee and a couple biscuits in our bellies, and by ten o'clock, we had nothing to show for our troubles.

It was nigh onto noon, with the sun overhead, when I heard another holler from Hobbes. I hustled over, then stared at what he was holding. He was wearing a grin from one ear to the other.

"I seen some tracks back over yonder," he said, pointing. "I knew we was gettin' close to the Rockwood station." He pointed again. I had seen it, too, a little farther down the line, a wooden shack and a water tower for the train to refuel.

"So," Hobbes said, "I taken my time with it when I seen them tracks, thinking he might have got a little careless, what with the train being so close, and all."

"And he was," I agreed, looking at the old bridle Hobbes was holding. On the ground, there was an old, beat-up saddle, lying there in the brush. Horse tracks led away from this spot.

I pushed my hat back on my head and took a long look toward the train shack at Rockwood station. The ground leading to the station was heavily forested with pine and fir, but right around the station was a grassy meadow, giving him a little cover and an easy approach. The station itself sat on a shelf, with the ground dropping away quickly from there to the Animas River.

It was getting pretty obvious our boy had hopped on the train here at Rockwood. What was I going to do about that?

I spread the three of us out in a line and walked the distance from where Hobbes and I were standing to the Rockwood station, looking around us as we went. Here and there, one of us called out when we saw a boot print.

It was Hobbes who saw the next important thing, and he hollered at me just like before. I was starting to think this guy was as good as a bloodhound. I hustled over there with the other militia man and found Hobbes standing just behind a big stack of firewood.

"Boot prints and knee prints," he said. "He was

hunkered down in back of this wood stack, just watchin' 'em over there."

I stood beside Hobbes and looked over the woodpile toward the station. I knew Hobbes was right. Scarface had picked this spot to watch the crew at work when the train rolled in.

I tried to picture the crew supplying the train with water and coal while this guy tried to hop on board with nobody seeing him. Getting into a boxcar would have been pretty hard, and somebody would have noticed him for sure in a passenger car. He maybe could have gotten out of this station on an open-sided gondola car, but I didn't think he could get to Silverton without being seen.

Then I thought about climbing to the roof and riding on top of the train. I had to laugh a little at that one. You could have to be crazy to ride the top on this line. The twisting, narrow rail lines through mountains and canyons—nobody would try that.

Well, we had done about all we could do here. I looked overhead and figured it was about noon. We needed to get back to Durango, where I could ask the folks some questions at the railroad. It was a half-day ride back to town, but I had a better idea. The train would come through here soon and it would stop at this station. My badge ought to be good enough to get us a ride.

"Take a seat and take it easy, boys," I told the militiamen. "We're gonna get home the easy way."

EIGHTEEN
HIDING OUT

The toe in his ribs caused Warner to roll away, swinging his fist at the legs of the man standing over him. A powerful arm reached down to yank him to his feet. Warner grabbed at his pistol, but his attacker stepped down on the gun, pinning Warner's hand to the floor of the boxcar. He yelped in pain and yanked his hand away.

The man shoved him away, and Warner felt himself stumbling toward the side of the boxcar, then reeling from a second strong shove. He had enough light coming through the side of the boxcar door to see a railroad uniform, so this must be the conductor. A very big, very strong conductor who seemed to enjoy dishing out punishment.

"What're you doin' here, boyo?" Warner could smell the whiskey on the conductor's breath. The tone of the question told him he was in for some more rough treatment.

Warner felt the man's elbow under his chin,

pressing his neck against the boxcar wall. He slid his hand down toward his belt, hoping there was a weapon within reach. The iron bar he had used to pry open the boxes and drawers at the bank was still there.

"Needed some sleep and a ride to Silverton. Hopped on at Rockwood. I'll pay," Warner offered. His voice was a squeak, and his breath came in gasps as the conductor kept leaning and shutting off his air. Warner would have to act soon, before his strength was completely gone.

"You're gonna be getting real sleepy soon, boyo," the conductor sneered. "Then I'll just go and have a look at what's in that bag you brought with you, boyo."

Warner felt himself fading. The surrounding sights in the boxcar were swimming. He yanked the iron bar from his belt and plunged the point into the conductor's side just as hard as he could. The man let out an oath and went to his knees. He gathered himself and let out a roar as he came off the ground.

Warner swung down with the bar and landed a lucky blow. The full force of the iron bar landed on the conductor's temple as he staggered up. He plunged to the floor and stayed there, face down.

Warner felt his attacker's neck for a heartbeat, then kicked the man several times in the ribs. Satisfied that the conductor was dead, he slumped to the floor of the boxcar and stayed there until his ragged breathing came back to normal.

Warner moved to the door and slid it open just enough to get a better look at the man who had almost killed him. He wasn't as big as Warner had thought, but the man had been incredibly strong. He left the door cracked open for some air and tried to get a grip on where they were. How long had he been asleep?

Warner struggled to his feet and walked back over to collect the gunny sack with his money. He felt around on the floor of the boxcar until he found his pistol, which he put back in his holster. He walked back over to the boxcar door and slid down to his rest on his haunches.

———

Warner sat up as he saw an approaching stop. There was a name on the water tank. He strained to read it. He knew the names of the stops and which ones took on passengers. He needed a stop for fuel only in order to slip away. His heart sank when he read the name *Needleton* on the water tank. Besides being a fuel stop, the train sometimes took on passengers here, mainly miners. If there were passengers, they would be looking for the conductor.

Warner pressed himself against the side of the boxcar and watched as the crew sprang into action, loading coal and swinging the water tender over the engine. He saw nobody trying to board.

The train pulled away after refueling with no new passengers. That bought him a little more time. Elk Park was the next stop, and that wasn't a passenger stop. After that, they would be in Silverton.

When the Needleton stop was out of sight, Warner stood and prepared to roll the dead conductor off the train. He grabbed the man by the lapels and pulled him up, finding him to be surprisingly heavy. He eased the body back to the floor and thought things over.

The uniform was a little too big for Warner, but not by that much. Warner was a big man himself. If he wore that uniform, maybe he could ride all the way to Silverton and slip away unnoticed. A man in a railroad uniform, even if he were seen hopping from a boxcar, wouldn't seem that out of place. From there, he could steal a horse in town and get away to his hideout at the abandoned mine tunnel.

In a matter of ten minutes, he was wearing the conductor's uniform. He grabbed his own clothes and stuffed them in the gunnysack. As the train climbed toward the Elk Park stop, he rolled the boxcar door farther open and shoved the dead body over the edge. It rolled and bounced for a good fifty yards before it came to a stop against a fir tree.

The final run into Silverton didn't take long. When they slowed at the station, he kept the sliding door pulled almost shut. Warner watched through the narrow opening at the crowd waiting to board. There were several passengers there. He prepared to leave quickly, because it wouldn't be long before they would need the conductor to present their tickets.

When the train came to a stop at the siding, Warner hopped out of the boxcar and strode away quickly, carrying the gunnysack over his shoulder. He heard someone call out a name, but he kept going without looking back. He didn't know the conductor's name, anyway. He had no idea who they were calling, and he wouldn't stick around to find out.

Five blocks down the street, he found a nice bay gelding tethered to the rail outside a saloon. In the saddle, there was a Winchester sticking out of the scabbard. No doubt the owner was inside, cutting his thirst. Warner wasted no time. Still wearing the railroad uniform, he swung aboard the gelding and rode away quickly.

When he passed through the miner's shantytown, he kept his head down and his eyes straight ahead. Somebody could recognize him here, and that would be trouble. He had killed two men here not too long ago. He didn't stop until he reached his hideout.

Once at the old mining cave, he took stock of what he had. He had the Winchester and a total of six bullets. At dusk, he shot a doe and made himself a campfire. He would decide tomorrow if he needed more supplies and how to get them if he did. For now, he had enough.

I made my way through the train cars, holding on while we rounded bends, until I reached the engine. I needed to talk to the engineer. I had to shout to make myself heard, but it couldn't be helped. I was in a hurry for some answers. More than a day had gone by already since the Durango robbery.

He glanced over at me and shrugged when I asked if we could talk.

"Suit yerself."

I leaned in and shouted. "You're the same crew

that made the run from Durango to Silverton yesterday, right?"

He glanced over again and nodded.

"Anything unusual happen yesterday? Could somebody have hopped the train at one of the stops?"

He shook his head, then shrugged. "Don't think so. Hard to say fer sure, 'cause the conductor didn't rightly do his job when we got to Silverton. He wasn't there, checkin' things over as folks got off, I mean. He woulda been the one to notice if somebody got themselves a free ride."

I wondered how long the conductor had been missing. "Was he there when you got to Silverton?"

"Yeah, he was there when we pulled in. I seen him. Seen the back of him, anyway. He was headed off into town in a hurry, seemed like. He weren't there last night at the boardin' house we use in Silverton, neither. Didn't show up fer work today. The railroad gave us another conductor for this trip."

I sat back and let that run through my head for a while. "You said you saw the back of him in Silverton yesterday?"

He nodded, then concentrated on his job for a minute as we rounded a bend and started to climb. "Yep, I seen the back of him, walkin' away. I hollered at him that we wasn't done here, but he kep' goin'." He shook his head. "Tain't like him to do that way."

I leaned in again. There was one thing I had to be sure of. "Are you for sure that was him? Couldn't have just been somebody about his size with a railroad uniform?"

He thought that one over. "Huh. Didn't think

about that." He stared out the window for a minute, then shook his head. "Nope, I can't be sure about that. He was big, just like Mick, and his hair was dark, but no, I can't be sure."

I stood up to leave, then thought of something else. "Did Mick live in Durango? He got a wife or family there?"

"Yep, got him a wife and a couple kids. Dunno exackly where he lives, but I guess somebody with the railroad could tell you."

I went back and plopped down into a seat next to the militiamen. I answered their question before they could ask.

"Coulda jumped the train yesterday at Rockwood," I said, "but it's pretty hard to say because the conductor from yesterday disappeared." I shook my head and stared out the window. "I'll have to ask around when we get back to Durango."

━━

I knew from my early days after returning to Colorado several years ago that the railroad kept an office in Durango. It was where I had first been hired by the railroad, several years back. When I went over to the office and showed the marshal's badge, it didn't take very long to get an address for Mick Kelly, the conductor. I rode over to his house directly from the railroad office.

A lady, maybe about forty, opened the door when I knocked. I remembered to take off my hat.

"Ma'am? I'm Marshal Smith. I've been trying to

find your husband, Mick. Do you know where he might be?"

She opened the door farther, and I could see the worry on her face now. "No!" she said immediately. "I took the horse and buggy to pick him up at the station, same as I always do. They said he wasn't on the train coming back. This hasn't happened before. Not ever."

I stepped aside as two small boys dashed past me and into the house. She reached out to grab my arm. "What's happening, Marshal?"

I had to admit I didn't know. "I'm going to ask around a little more here in Durango," I told her. "Then I'll probably have to go up to Silverton to see what I can find out. Nobody seems to know where he went yesterday after the train got to Silverton."

She nodded, saying nothing. I put my hat back on and stepped away. "Just as soon as I know something, I'll tell you," I promised.

I stopped off at the telegraph office and found several messages waiting for me. I looked them over. The biggest thing I saw was about a street fight in Leadville between some miners and some locals. There was another telegram there about a little rustling going on up near Pueblo. I would have to send Hardison, so I went looking for him.

I found Hardison in a café on Main Street. He and his boys hadn't found out anything about the disappearing outlaw, but I told him I was pretty sure our guy had hopped the train going north at the Rockwood station. I couldn't say what that had to do with a missing conductor, but I was pretty sure those things were tied together.

Hardison mostly listened and waited, like he always did. Then he asked what he always did after I got done talking.

"What can I do?"

I passed over the telegrams about the Leadville problem and the rustling. "Take care of these," I told him. "I just need one other thing."

He nodded and waited. "Let me take Hobbs with me. I'm gonna need a tracker, and that guy could track a ghost through a dust storm."

___

I sank into a seat at the *Suds 'n Such* and grinned when Holt came over and plunked a beer down in front of me. He had another for Hobbs. I said it was on the house, but I was thinking that was a mistake when I saw how fast he sucked it down. I decided I would cut him off after two beers.

Sarge came in after twenty minutes, which saved me the trouble of looking for him. I needed his help too, not just as the sheriff, but as my friend. He sat and listened while I filled him in on the Durango robbery and the escape of the outlaw with the deep scar on his face.

Sarge pushed his beer glass around the table while he thought. "First thing, I guess, is to look for this missing conductor," he said. "I can check the boardinghouses. We've got a couple of hotels, too. I can check those, but I doubt we will find him there. Too expensive."

"We'll help," I told him. Another thought hit me. "If this guy hopped the train and made it to Silverton," I said, "whether he got rid of the conductor and took his uniform or not, he'd arrive here in town without a horse. I don't expect he'd paid for one, neither."

Sarge grinned and shook his head a little. "That's why you've gotta keep wearin' that badge, Lat. You're too good at this." He nodded. "Yep, we had a horse stolen yesterday afternoon. Right about the time that train got to town, too. Somebody took it right from in front of a saloon, cool as you please. We haven't found it yet."

He looked across the table at Hobbs, who was staring sadly at the bottom of his empty glass.

"Don't buy him one," I said. "We've got to go, and anyway, you ain't never seen a beer disappear so fast."

Sarge chuckled and stood. "That horse was a bay gelding, about five years old. I'll give you the name of the brand on him. I've got it written down at the office. You boys wanna split up the boardinghouses and start looking?"

And that's what we did, but two hours later, we were back at the *Suds 'n Such*, not knowing any more than we had when we left. I thanked Sarge and gave Hobbs some money for a boardinghouse. It was time for me to get home to see my wife and baby boy.

◼

After a while, it wasn't so much the food Warner wanted in his hideout. Yes, he was tired of venison after two meals, but he wasn't going hungry. There was a trout stream nearby, but he at least needed some string and a hook. Maybe some cornmeal to fry up would be good.

Mainly, though, it was more about the firepower. He had stolen a horse with a Winchester on it, but that Winchester was the 1866 Yellow Boy. He had only five cartridges left after bringing down the buck. That wasn't nearly enough. Really, he needed a Winchester 73 and several dozen rounds of ammunition. He had a few rounds for his Colt, but he needed more. And a shotgun would help if they charged his position here. Plus, a good knife. If they came after him, he would give them a hot reception.

On the second morning, Warner decided he would have to make a trip to the general store at the edge of town. He saddled up the bay gelding and started early, making sure to avoid the paths that would take him through the miner's shantytown. He didn't need people seeing him and talking about him.

That just left the owner of the run-down general store to worry about. Warner had a feeling in his gut that he couldn't trust that guy to keep his mouth shut. There was really only one solution to a problem like that. Warner had no problems with that solution.

There was one other horse at the hitching rail out front when Warner arrived. A quick glance through the window confirmed there was just one customer in the store. He pretended to tend the right rear hoof of his horse while he waited for the customer to finish up and get out.

Finally, the store was empty except for the owner. Warner strode through the door and wasted no time. He told the owner to get out a shotgun, a Winchester 73, a good hunting knife, and lots of ammo, including Colt 45 ammo. When the man's eyebrows climbed up into his forehead, Warner knew he couldn't leave the man alive. No chance this guy wouldn't talk about all the weapons he was buying. Besides, Warner had no intention of paying.

When the guns were all on the counter, Warner told the man to get him some cornmeal, fishing line, several cans each of beans and peaches, and some jerky. The man hurried to get those items and bring them back. Warner checked the guns, sighting down the barrels, while he waited. Satisfied, he watched the owner stack the additional items on the counter.

Warner told the man he needed to get a sack to carry his purchases and stepped outside while the owner slowly added up the total. Warner checked up and down the street. It was empty.

Stepping back inside, the man presented the total bill. Warner pretended to check it while the man looked for the sack Warner said he'd gone to get.

"No sack," he told Warner.

Warner's hand closed over the hunting knife on the counter while he pointed behind the man. "What about that one?" he asked.

The owner turned, puzzled. "What are you talking about?"

Warner leaned over the counter and struck with

the knife, then smothered the man's cries with his left hand while he lowered him slowly to the floor. Warner helped himself to a second scabbard from the store and loaded the guns and supplies on the gelding. He again took the long route around the miner's shanty-town on the way back to his cave.

NINETEEN
ON THE TRAIL

I met up with Sarge and with Hobbs, my tracker, at the bakery in Silverton early the next morning. There was a time when we'd have met at my house, with Joanna baking up a storm for us, but having baby Ethan around the place had changed everything. Joanna had her hands full these days, so we did the next best thing, meeting at Joanna's old bakery for breakfast.

Hobbs was already working on his second plate of eggs when Sarge came through the door and took a seat. He told us he had swung by Mick the engineer's house last night, and Mick had never come home. He'd not been seen around town, either. Sarge had asked around about that, too, with the same results.

I was afraid I knew what that meant. Mick was likely lying dead somewhere along the railroad tracks between here and Durango, and somebody else had been wearing his uniform when the train pulled in at Silverton.

"Your call," Sarge said. "What do you wanna do now?"

I looked across the table at Hobbs. "You're gonna have to earn your money for some tracking now," I told him. "We'll have to backtrack from Silverton, back down the line toward Durango. If he's still alive, he's gonna need our help."

Hobbs nodded and pushed away his empty plate. "How far back do you wanna track?" he asked. "There's a lot of places he couldn't have survived a fall off that train, when you git up over some of those peaks."

I sipped the last of my coffee and thought that one over. "We'll check as far back as Needleton," I said. "If nothing turns up by then, we'll have to assume he didn't make it and come back here to start the search for that Durango bank robber."

I thought for another second. "I'll have Captain Hardison check around on the Durango side for the conductor if we can't find anything on this end."

I turned to Sarge. "You can start looking around town here for that bank robber," I said. "There's still a missing horse that might have something to do with all this. Maybe out around the miner's shantytown they've seen something."

———

We parted ways in front of the bakery and agreed to meet here again in two days if we hadn't seen each other before then. I waited outside Hobbs's boarding-house while he packed up for a trip, then we started working our way south from the train station in Silverton.

For the first two miles, we stayed on horseback, working back and forth between the tracks and the Animas River on one side. On the far side, the ground was free enough of trees and brush that we stayed on horseback over there, too.

Two miles out, we had to dismount and lead the horses, looking in the brush and moving back and forth through the pines and firs, searching for any signs of a man thrown from the train—broken branches, skid marks in the needles on the forest floor, or scavengers gathering.

We worked another two miles on foot along the train tracks. The air was cold enough that I could see my breath—we were still almost at nine thousand feet —but I felt the sweat start to pour down my neck.

I called a break and sat down with Hobbs to eat the lunch they had packed for us at the bakery. I swigged down some cold water and stared off to the south. Hobbs followed my gaze.

"How far to that station at Elk Park?"

I took one more swig of the water and stuffed it back into my pack. "About another mile or two," I estimated. "We can search on up to the Elk Park station today and start working toward Needleton if we don't see anything. We can make camp after that."

We were just about in the shadow of the station at Elk Park when I heard a yell from Hobbs. I led my horse up the incline and over the tracks, working down in his direction. I was still about thirty yards away when I could see that Hobbs had found what we were looking for. There was a body wrapped around a fir tree down there.

Hobbs was standing several yards away and looking down the slope by the time I scrambled down to where he stood. I looked at the incline we had to cover with that body to get back up to the tracks. I told Hobbs I needed some help to get the body onto my horse.

Hobbs seemed to snap out of it and walked back to help me lift and secure the body on my horse. We walked the horses up the incline to the tracks.

"Just help me lead the horses back along the tracks to the station," I told Hobbs. "We can leave the body at the Elk Park station and let them put it on the train for his widow to bury. We can't leave him here."

In another thirty minutes, we had left the body at Elk Park with instructions for the crew to put it on the next train back to Silverton. By the time we had done that, I glanced up at the sun. It was late afternoon.

"That's all for today," I told Hobbs. "Tomorrow, we'll meet up with Sarge and see what he's found out today. We still have the bank robber to catch, only now it looks like he murdered a man, too."

◼︎━━◼︎

His freshly stolen horse balked before they reached the mouth of the abandoned mine tunnel. No amount of kicking him in the ribs or cursing could budge the animal. Warner dismounted with one last oath and led him away, leaving the horse in a small clearing outside the tunnel where there was enough brush for grazing.

Warner unloaded the food from the horse first. He didn't want the smell to attract predators. He carried the jerky and cornmeal into the tunnel, along with the cans of beans and peaches. He carried them to the far wall and stacked the cans, then tore open the jerky and pulled out a couple of sticks.

Warner froze in position when he heard a loud whinny from the horse outside, followed by the unmistakable screech of a mountain lion. He drew his Colt and ran to the mouth of the tunnel. The bay gelding was galloping away, following the faint trail Warner had taken from town. The gelding's left flank was bleeding.

Warner whirled and saw a large mountain lion chasing after the gelding. Holding his pistol in both hands, he centered his sights on the mountain lion's neck and squeezed off his shot. The predator stumbled, then dropped. He twitched twice, then lay still.

Warner squatted on his knees and let loose a fresh round of cursing. If he had tethered the horse, it would be dead, but he would still have the rifles and ammunition he had taken from the general store this morning. Now the horse was gone, and the weapons were gone with him.

Warner holstered his Colt and walked down to the mountain lion he'd just shot, prodding it with a stick to be sure the animal was dead. He stared at the big cat, wondering why it would attack a horse. Usually, they went after smaller game like deer, unless game was scarce.

He stood and paced back and forth on the trail. Whatever the reason, his horse was gone. He didn't have enough weapons and ammunition now to hold off an attack in the mine tunnel. An attacker with superior firepower could wear him down, leaving him fair game to be taken out with a sudden rush.

Worse, the horse might just run all the way back to town or maybe stop at the general store where he had been this morning. Either way, the gelding's tracks would leave a clear trail back to the mine tunnel. The weapons Warner had taken from the general store this morning would tie him directly to the dead man at the store. That would bring the law in a hurry. He had to move out now.

Warner wasted no more time on the runaway gelding or the dead mountain lion. He went back into the mine tunnel and bundled up his extra food and ammunition into his bedroll. When he left the tunnel, he automatically turned south, away from Silverton. He was looking for a place that he could defend from attack, as well as use for a hideout. Luckily, he knew that a lot of miners must have set up a shack or camping site around this area.

He worked his way down a steep incline, then followed a game trail for about a half mile until the game trail crossed a small, rushing mountain stream. Warner stopped, laid down the bedroll and the old Winchester, and looked around, gazing up the slope above him. This was the kind of place an old prospector might have used to put up a shanty while he worked.

Warner took his time, knowing that the place he was looking for was liable to blend in with the surroundings, tucked back into a notch in the mountain slopes or maybe dug into another old mining tunnel. His eyes settled on a gray, sagging structure about halfway up the slope. He hefted the bedroll onto his back, picked up the Winchester, and climbed up to find an abandoned miner's shack.

Warner set the bedroll down on the dirt floor. He already knew this place was as good a spot as he was likely to find in the time he had available. He could settle in here for a couple days and see whether the law was after him. If not, he could steal another horse back in town and be on his way.

There was a half-built rock fireplace along the back wall and a rusty old pick leaning against the wall in the corner. On a shelf along one wall were several cans of beans. Somebody had abandoned this place in a hurry. It could have been an Indian attack, or maybe a sudden snowstorm in the late fall that caused the miner to clear out.

There was a door in the front wall, but the wood all around it was crumbling. Still, it offered a little protection. He could shoot through the place that had been carved out of the door for a window. If there had ever been any glass, it was long gone.

He walked out and stood in front of the cabin, frowning for the first time. This site must have been chosen mainly for how close it was to the fresh water below, and maybe how close it was to wherever this guy was prospecting. As a defensive position, it wasn't great.

The cabin was about halfway up-slope, meaning an attacker could get around him to the higher ground.

Out in front, there was a level spot in the ground that was wider than he would have liked. An attacker could reach level ground in front of where Warner now stood and take cover behind a tree to lay down fire into the cabin. Warner wasn't kidding himself about how many shots these decaying old walls would stop.

Warner shook his head and went back inside the cabin. He made sure the old Winchester was loaded with as many cartridges as he had, then did the same with the Colt. He had enough ammo for about twenty-five shots.

━━━

We found Sarge at the café the next morning and joined him for breakfast. He agreed we were now looking for a murderer, not just a bank robber. My breakfast hadn't arrived yet when a guy burst in through the front door, hollering that he needed the sheriff.

I spun around to take a look, and I didn't know this guy. Sarge didn't seem to know him either. He was dressed like a miner, but his boots were scuffed and worn down, and there were patched up holes in his britches.

"Betcha he's livin' out there in the miner's shanty-town," I muttered to Sarge.

He nodded and waved to the guy, pointing at his badge and standing up. "I'm the sheriff," he barked.

The miner dashed across the café and skidded to a stop in front of our table. "You gotta come, Sarge," he gasped. "It's Henry down at the general store. The one near the miner's town, I mean. He's been kilt."

Sarge glanced over at me, then back at the miner. "Where? I mean, where did you see him? Are you sure he's dead?"

The man started back toward the door, waving his arms at Sarge. "Yeah, I'm sure. Ol' Henry done been filleted like a fish. You gotta come."

Sarge dug into his pocket and came out with money for his breakfast. The waiter came out of the kitchen with food for Hobbs and me, but I waved him off and followed Sarge out to our horses. Hobbs was behind me, and we mounted up to ride out to the miner's shantytown.

There was a crowd around *Henry's General Store* when we rode up. They were all outside the store. Nobody seemed to want to be inside, and I could see why after I went in and looked behind the counter. There was no doubt that Henry was dead. Hobbs took one look and went back outside. I found a blanket on one of the shelves and tossed it over the corpse. This made two dead men in two days, and I had a feeling the same guy had done both.

Sarge looked relieved when I covered the body. "You reckon this guy got killed this morning?" he asked.

I nodded. "Henry might not have done a lot of business out here, but I reckon somebody would have found him sooner if it had happened before this mornin'."

Sarge nodded. "I'll get somebody to come out and fetch the body," he said. "He's prob'ly got some family around here somewhere. I'll let 'em know."

I walked around behind the counter and found a cash box on a shelf down there. I opened it. "Huh," was all I had to say.

Sarge walked around and joined me, looking into the box. "Whoever killed Henry didn't take the money," he observed. He looked around. "Why would he have killed this poor guy if it wasn't a robbery?"

I stood and looked around. "Do you think maybe we could tell if the killer took anything?" I was kinda thinkin' out loud, but I started to walk around. "I mean, if we see empty spots at the front of a shelf, maybe that's something the guy took."

I was staring at the gun racks high on the wall behind the counter. There was a ladder leaning against the wall nearby, and there were two empty spots on the gun racks. Sarge moved toward the gun racks and mouthed what I was thinking.

"Shotgun missing," he murmured, "and a Winchester 73 rifle."

I walked over and looked at the boxes of ammunition stacked on shelves below the gun racks. "Looks like he got some shotgun shells," I added, then took a look under the Winchester 73 rack. ".44 cartridges for the Winchester, too," I added. There was another empty spot on the ammunition shelves, and I moved down to look.

"Looks like maybe he's got a little extra ammo for a

Colt 45 now, too," I said. This guy was loaded to the gills for a fight.

Sarge and I walked out of the store and pulled the doors shut behind us. Sarge walked over to a group of people standing outside, and I heard him ask if Henry had any family. I moved over to where Hobbs was standing and caught him up on what we had seen inside.

I was wondering if we had enough firepower to match up with this guy when we found him. I looked over at Hobbes.

"Whaddya think, if we find this guy. Will he be forted-up?"

"Yep. Likely."

"Yeah." I looked over at the store, then back at Hobbs. "What would you use if you were outgunned and the guy you're after is behind walls or a fort of some kind with all that firepower?"

Hobbs leaned over and spit, then grinned just a little. "Mind you, I'm from Tennessee. We've been known to use dynamite."

I nodded and looked over at the store. "Hold on," I said. "I'll be back."

It took me no time at all to find two sticks of dynamite and a box of matches. I left some money in the cash box to pay for it. Henry's kinfolk would own this place now, and I wouldn't short them for the dynamite. I walked out and put the dynamite and matches in my saddlebag.

After a while, Sarge came over and pulled me aside. "Henry had a brother and some kinfolks down the road just a piece," he told me. "I'm going over now to tell them about this. I'll get somebody to come and get the body, too. What are you gonna do?"

I turned and looked at the trail leading to the miner's shantytown and beyond that, the faint trail that followed the path of the railroad. "We're gonna scout out yonder for a while," I said, pointing toward shantytown. "We'll ask around the shantytown and see if Hobbs can pick up any tracks going south from there toward Durango."

Hobbs and I were just about to gather the reins and saddle up when I heard a commotion behind me on the trail leading into town. I turned around to see a couple of the guys who had been in front of the general store flagging down a riderless horse. It looked like a bay gelding.

I moved out to get a closer look at the horse. It was a bay gelding, just like I'd thought, and it had claw marks across its flank. Most likely from a mountain lion, from what I could tell. He had a saddle and bridle on him. I held the reins and soothed him, looking at what he was carrying.

There were two scabbards. One held a Winchester 73, and the other held a double-barreled shotgun. A look in the saddlebag showed me a lot of ammunition. I let out a low whistle. I turned when Hobbs walked up beside me.

"Looks like we found the horse the general store robber was riding," I told him. "And if I'm not mistaken, this horse fits the description of the one stolen just a day or two ago in town."

I looked at the two guys who were holding the horse. "When the sheriff comes back, tell him these look like the guns stolen from this store. He'll probably agree that this horse was stolen in town yesterday. Tell him Lat Smith and Hobbs are going to see if we can backtrack this horse."

They nodded. Hobbs and I mounted up and moved south out of town, heading for shantytown and the rail lines south.

TWENTY
WARNER'S STAND

The gelding's tracks were clear enough all the way back to shantytown, but there they just blended in with other traffic on the trail. I watched Hobbs work at figuring it out for a while, then called it off.

"Let's just see if we can pick 'em up on the other side of shantytown," I told him. "That's likely to be where he came from."

Sure enough, on the trail running toward the railroad tracks, we picked up the gelding's tracks again and followed them to a small clearing. There were flecks of blood on some rocks along the way, so this looked like the place where he had been clawed. If that wasn't enough, Hobbs whistled and pointed out a dead mountain lion at the side of the trail.

I whistled, too, and knelt beside the dead predator. Somebody had shot him clean through the neck. I looked a little farther. There had been only the one shot.

We explored a little around that clearing and came across what looked like an abandoned mining tunnel. We stayed clear of the entrance and checked around to both sides. Somebody had left some boot prints here, and they looked pretty recent.

"I don't cotton to the idea of stickin' my head into that tunnel," Hobbs said. "Somebody got off a mighty good shot at that big cat over there. I don't feel like givin' him a shot at me."

"Nope," I agreed.

"Dynamite?" he asked.

I thought that one over long and hard, then shook my head. "We don't know if there's anybody in there, and if there is, we don't know who. No, I'll try something else."

We moved to opposite sides of the entrance and flattened ourselves against the outer wall. I pulled a match from my pocket, lit it, and chucked it into the tunnel. It slowly burned out. We heard nothing.

Next, I cupped my hands and yelled into the tunnel.

"If there's anybody in there," I hollered, "I'm fixin' to fire several shots into the walls all around you. If you've ever seen anybody soak up some ricochets, you know it ain't pretty. I'm givin' you thirty seconds to come out with yore hands up."

I lit another match, threw it, and waited. Nothing. After a while, I lit another one and threw it, then ducked into the tunnel and pressed myself against a wall. The match burned out and I waited, not daring to move. My eyes started to adjust to the dim light. I waited and watched.

I moved slowly along the wall, deeper into the tunnel, then I lit another match and tossed it. This time, I could see all the way to the back. The tunnel was empty. I called to Hobbs and the two of us searched inside. Somebody had built a small fire in there within the last day or two, but it was empty now. There wasn't anything else to see.

We left the cave and Hobbs cast back and forth, looking for tracks. He found a set of them, leading down from the tunnel and to the south, following in the direction of the railroad tracks.

We left the horses tied up outside the cave, not sure if there was a trail wide enough to ride through where we were going. We could only hope that the dead mountain lion didn't have any friends still around. I grabbed my pack and brought it with me.

Hobbs took the lead, following the tracks down a steep incline and to a narrow game trail. We came to a mountain stream and Hobbs paused, looking for where our quarry might have crossed the stream.

He saw what he was looking for and waved, crossing the stream and pausing at the foot of another slight incline. Suddenly, a shot rang out and Hobbs fell to the ground, rolling behind a pine tree just in time as another shot followed the first. I dove behind a boulder at the edge of the stream.

"Hobbs!" I looked to my left and saw him behind a thick tree trunk, holding his right leg. "How bad is it?"

"Not sure," he said between clenched teeth. "Went through. Don't think it's broke. Just not sure. I dunno if I can walk. For sure, I can't move fast to be much help."

I couldn't see much above the bank of the stream, just in front of me. I was pretty sure I was below the shooter's line of vision, but I didn't want to stick my fool head up to find out. I tossed a rock into some brush above me and off to my right. A bullet tore through the place where it landed immediately.

I pulled the dynamite and the matches from my pack and checked to see that my Colt was loaded. I looked over at Hobbes. "I'm gonna work to my right," I told him. "I can follow the stream bed for a while and stay down low enough. He's got us pinned unless I can flank him."

Hobbes nodded and braced himself against the trunk of the tree. His Winchester was beside him, and his Colt was in his lap. I just hoped he could stay conscious.

I moved out to my right, keeping low and trying to stay silent and not start any branches moving up where he might be able to see them. I took my time, but I was worried about Hobbs. I couldn't take all day.

After about fifteen minutes, I figured I had gone thirty yards, moving to my right and a little bit uphill. It was time to risk a look over the creek bank. I had to know where this guy was. I moved up behind a fir tree and lifted my head ever so slowly, then stood and eased out from behind the tree for a look.

Now I could see it. At least, I could see the place where I thought he was forted up. It looked like an old, falling-down miner's shack, built snug up against the hillside. The wood looked rotted out in a few places. I studied it, my eyes roving over the front wall, then coming to a stop at the door. There was a rifle barrel sticking out through some kind of notch in the door. I could see about three inches of barrel.

"Gotcha," I breathed.

He still had a good enough angle that he might see me if I stepped out to throw the dynamite from here. I ducked back down and wormed my way around for another fifteen yards. Now, I decided, was the time. I hoped I was out of his line of vision. I pulled a stick of dynamite and a match from my bag and gathered my feet under me. I was sure I could reach that shack with the dynamite if I made a good throw from here.

I struck the match, lit the dynamite, came to my feet, and stepped out from behind a tree. I heaved the dynamite and watched it sail end over end toward the shack. I dropped back behind the tree and waited.

The explosion was louder than I expected. The ground shook for a moment and I stayed down, my hands over my ears. Then I scrambled to my feet and stared. I hadn't hit the front door, but I got close. There was a hole in the front wall just a couple feet away from the door.

While I watched, the door collapsed and a man came staggering out, pawing at his eyes and reeling away from the shack.

"Hey!" I stepped out from the trees, Colt in hand. "Drop to your knees!" I yelled. "I'm too close to miss."

He twisted his head slowly to look at me, and even from here, I could see the scar on his cheek. He didn't move, just stared at me.

"You've got your piece in yer hand and I don't," he snarled. "Where I come from, a man gets a fair chance."

Well, I wasn't thinking he deserved a fair chance. I doubt either of the men he killed got a fair chance. Anyway, I was just going to arrest him if he would come quietly. Still, something in me wanted to end this thing now.

I didn't say a word. I just slowly dropped my Colt back into the holster. He let loose with an evil-sounding cackle, then crouched down low, turned, and drew.

My Colt was in my hand as soon as he started moving. I fired and hit him dead center in the chest, but I felt a burning across my right side at the same moment, and he was still holding the gun, staggering back and lifting it for another shot.

I took a small step to my right and fired again. He took the second shot in the center of his chest again. His second shot went wild over my head, but he was somehow still on his feet, trying to line up another shot.

I fired twice more, and he stumbled back and went down. I stared for a long time, wondering how he had stayed on his feet that long. I heard a small noise to my left and whirled, then relaxed.

Sarge was standing at the edge of the clearing, holding up Hobbs, who was balanced on his one good leg, gun in hand.

"I been lookin' for you boys," Sarge said. "You sure do make a lot of noise."

Somehow, even after the explosion at the cabin, there had been a gunny sack in there, unharmed and still full of money, lying against the back wall. After Sarge and I had got back to Silverton and dropped off Hobbs at the doc's office, the first thing I had done was to put that money on the train to Silverton.

Sarge said he would get a couple guys to bury Scarface out there on the mountain, and that was good enough for me. I certainly didn't have any good words to say over him. I didn't even care what his name was.

I had kept it to myself about holstering my Colt to give that guy a fair chance. I wasn't sorry I had done it, but I didn't want to have to explain it. Especially not to Joanna.

Speaking of Joanna, that's how I found myself on a cot in the doc's office, just a room over from Hobbs right now. She had gotten word I was back in town, and she had hustled me over to the doc when she saw that furrow along my right hip. The doc said it wasn't dangerous, but it was deep. So, I was gonna be his guest here for a couple days.

Doc had just got done pokin' and proddin' and trussing me all up like a mummy. Lying on my back was the only comfortable thing, so that's what I was doing. Then the door opened, and Joanna came through. She took a seat on the side of my bed.

"Doc says you're going to be fine," she said, taking my hand. "You just have to stay here for a while."

"I know," I said. I knew what she would say next, so I just waited for it.

She took my hand. "You're not just a husband anymore," she pointed out. "You're a dad. We both need you. You have to say no if they ask you about staying on as marshal. Ethan and I can't have you out there getting shot at anymore."

"I will. I promise." I had already thought about it, and the family and the ranch were what mattered. There would be somebody to step in and enforce the law. My badge was lying on top of my bag at the side of the bed. I had already decided I wouldn't be putting that back on.

"I'm done with it," I said. "I'll send the badge back to the governor."

"Good." She leaned over to give me a kiss. "The governor is coming to see you tomorrow. You can tell him yourself. Don't forget your promise." Then she left, telling me she would be back after I had got a little sleep.

I could hear Hobbs in the room next door, so when the doc left to make his rounds, I pulled myself up off the cot and walked around the corner to see Hobbs. He looked as bored as I felt, but I think he kinda brightened up when I plopped down in a chair next to his cot.

"How you doin'?" I asked. "You gonna be okay after some rest?"

"That's what the doc says." Hobbs nodded. "He says I gotta stay here for another couple of days, then use a cane and keep the weight off that leg for a while. Bullet went right through it, though. Didn't break the leg."

"Good," I said. "Hardison will be glad to get you back."

Hobbs shook his head. "Naw, my time is up. I

signed up for two years and it's done now. I'm gonna do something else, I reckon." He glanced at me sideways. "I've worked cattle a time or two. I know a little about it."

I leaned forward, then moaned a little and leaned back. Moving was painful. "I've got a ranch, right outside of town," I said. "If you want a ranch job, I'd be glad to have you."

He grinned. "That's what I've been hopin' for."

We shook on the deal, then I heard the front door opening. I scooted back to my cot before the doc could catch me.

By the next morning, I had worn the doc down, asking when I could get out. He told me I could go by noon if everything looked okay after he saw a couple of patients this morning.

I was dozing off, waiting for the doc to get back, when I heard somebody come into the room and take a seat. I opened my eyes and saw that Joanna had been right. It was Governor Pritkin. He had come to see me, just like she said.

I stared. "What're you doin' here?" was the smartest thing I could think of to ask.

He chuckled. "Good to see you too, Lat. I was in Durango yesterday on some business and heard how you caught the last of the bank robber gang and got the money back for the bank in Durango. I came up to see how you're doing and to ask you a question."

Well, I was pretty sure what that question would

be, and I had already made a promise to Joanna, but I waited to hear him out.

He leaned forward. "Colorado's growing, Lat," he said. "We've got lots of silver and gold, lots of cattle ranches, and lots of new businesses. What we need is to make it a good, safe, honest place for everyone. Good for cattle ranchers, good for businessmen, and good for families. We need you to help us with that. You're one of the best lawmen I've ever seen. I've come to ask you to make that marshal's job permanent."

I squirmed a little on the cot, trying to find the best words. Finally, I just spat it out. "I can't do it," I said. "I made a promise to my wife, Joanna, to hang up the badge. We've got us a little baby boy now, and I promised I would just be a rancher. That's what I want to do, and I keep my promises."

The governor sat back and nodded. "I had a feeling you would say that, but I had to try." He looked out the window for a minute, then turned back to me. "Who can you recommend, then, if it can't be you?"

"Hardison," I said. "Captain Hardison of the state militia. He's a good man. He'll do you proud."

"Hardison. Okay." He stood and put on his hat, then reached out his hand to shake mine. "You rest and get well."

On the way out of my room, he passed by Joanna, coming in to see me with baby Ethan. She came to sit down beside me, looking out the door. "Who was that?"

"That was the governor, came to see me, just like you said," I told her. "He wanted me to stay on as a marshal, but I turned him down. I'm gonna live a quiet life now and be a rancher and stay out of trouble."

She laughed, put Ethan down to explore the cot, and leaned over to give me a kiss. "Well," she said, "I believe everything except the part about staying out of trouble."

Half an hour later, she helped me into the wagon, and I was on my way home to the ranch I had built. Come to think of it, the ranch was outside a town I had helped to build, in a new state I had helped to build. It all felt pretty good.

A LOOK AT

NASH WALKER: FEUD ON THE FRONTIER (NASH WALKER 1)

He came to Texas to outrun his past. What he found was a war he couldn't walk away from.

In the rugged aftermath of heartbreak, Nash Walker, a hardened moonshiner from the hills of Tennessee, rides west with nothing left to lose. Texas offers a chance at redemption —or ruin. From bounty hunter to reluctant Texas Ranger, Nash is soon swept into the bloody Sutton-Taylor feud, one of the deadliest range wars in frontier history.

When an enchanting singer named Victoria pleads for help protecting her family's land from a ruthless neighbor and his gang of hired guns, Nash can't turn his back. With bullets flying and loyalties tested, he'll need the grit of a frontiersman, the law of a Ranger, and the backing of cattle baron Charles Goodnight to survive.

Will Nash find peace on the Texas frontier, or will this new fight cost him everything he has left?

AVAILABLE NOVEMBER 2025

ABOUT THE AUTHOR

Patrick Lindsay came to Texas by way of Missouri, Canada, and California and has been proud to call the Lone Star State his home for more than forty years now. He retired in 2017 from "another life" as a CPA, whereafter he turned his hand to writing.

He has read just about everything by Louis L'Amour and first decided to give Western writing a try on his initial day of retirement. He has been writing ever since and loves the idea that so many people get enjoyment from his work.

Patrick and his wife Michelle live on a cattle ranch near Fort Worth along with cows, horses, chickens, and a very spoiled Great Pyrenees dog. He is an avid fan of the St. Louis Cardinals in baseball and the Kansas City Chiefs in football.